Nights

William Trevor was born in M⎯⎯⎯⎯⎯⎯⎯⎯⎯ ⎯⎯⎯⎯⎯ f
a bank official, and spent his c⎯⎯⎯⎯⎯ ⎯⎯⎯⎯⎯⎯ ⎯⎯⎯⎯. He studied
at Trinity College, Dublin. Working first as a sculptor and teacher, then
as an advertising copywriter, he published his first novel in 1958.

His subsequent novels have won numerous prizes, including the
Hawthornden Prize, the Heinemann Fiction Prize and the *Yorkshire Post*
Book of the Year Award. He is a three-times winner of the Whitbread
Book of the Year Award, for *The Children of Dynmouth* (1976), *Fools of
Fortune* (1983) and *Felicia's Journey* (1994), and has also been shortlisted
four times for the Booker Prize, most recently for *The Story of Lucy Gault*
in 2002. His latest novel is *Love and Summer* (2009).

William Trevor is also an acclaimed writer of short stories. His
complete output was collected into two hardcover volumes by Viking
Penguin in 2009. In 1999 he was awarded the prestigious David Cohen
Prize for a lifetime's literary achievement, and in 2002 he was knighted
for his services to literature. He has lived in Devon for many years.

Nights at the Alexandra

WILLIAM TREVOR

PENGUIN BOOKS

PENGUIN BOOKS

Published by the Penguin Group
Penguin Books Ltd, 80 Strand, London WC2R 0RL, England
Penguin Group (USA) Inc., 375 Hudson Street, New York, New York 10014, USA
Penguin Group (Canada), 90 Eglinton Avenue East, Suite 700, Toronto, Ontario, Canada M4P 2Y3
(a division of Pearson Penguin Canada Inc.)
Penguin Ireland, 25 St Stephen's Green, Dublin 2, Ireland (a division of Penguin Books Ltd)
Penguin Group (Australia), 707 Collins Street, Melbourne, Victoria 3008, Australia
(a division of Pearson Australia Group Pty Ltd)
Penguin Books India Pvt Ltd, 11 Community Centre, Panchsheel Park, New Delhi – 110 017, India
Penguin Group (NZ), 67 Apollo Drive, Rosedale, Auckland 0632, New Zealand
(a division of Pearson New Zealand Ltd)
Penguin Books (South Africa) (Pty) Ltd, Block D, Rosebank Office Park,
181 Jan Smuts Avenue, Parktown North, Gauteng 2193, South Africa

Penguin Books Ltd, Registered Offices: 80 Strand, London WC2R 0RL, England

www.penguin.com

Nights at the Alexandra first published by Hutchinson 1987
'The Ballroom of Romance' first published 1972
'The Hill Bachelors' first published 2000
This collection first published in Penguin Books 2015

001

Copyright © William Trevor, 1972, 1987, 2000
All rights reserved

The moral right of the author has been asserted

Set in 11/13 pt Dante MT Std
Typeset by Jouve (UK), Milton Keynes
Printed in Great Britain by Clays Ltd, St Ives plc

ISBN: 978-0-241-96951-9

www.greenpenguin.co.uk

Contents

Nights at the Alexandra

I

I am a fifty-eight-year-old provincial. I have no children. I have never married.

'Harry, I have the happiest marriage in the world! Please, when you think of me, remember that.'

That is what I hear most often and with the greatest pleasure: Frau Messinger's voice as precisely recalled as memory allows, each quizzical intonation reflected in a glance or gesture. I must have replied something, Heaven knows what: it never mattered because she rarely listened. The war had upset the Messingers' lives, she being an Englishwoman and he German. It brought them to Ireland and to Cloverhill – a sanctuary they most certainly would not otherwise have known. She explained to me that she would not have found life comfortable in Hitler's Germany; and her own country could hardly be a haven for her husband. They had thought of Switzerland, but Herr Messinger believed that Switzerland would be invaded; and the United States did not tempt them. No one but I, at that time an unprepossessing youth of fifteen, ever used their German titles: in the town where I'd been born they were Mr and Mrs Messinger, yet it seemed to me – affectation, I daresay – that in this way we should honour the strangers that they were.

When first I heard of the Messingers I had just returned from the Reverend Wauchope's rectory, where I lodged in term-time in order to attend Lisscoe grammar school. My father told me about them. He said the man was twice the woman's age; he imagined they were Jews since they attended no church. A lot of Jews had slipped away from Germany, he ponderously added.

As a matter of principle, I refused to be interested in anything my father related, but a few days later I saw Frau Messinger

3

stepping out of her husband's motor-car in Laffan Street and guessed at once who she was. The motor-car was powered by propane gas, a complicated apparatus being mounted where part of the luggage compartment had been removed: no one had petrol to spare during what in Ireland we called the 'Emergency', and energy so ingeniously contrived was rare. A group of loiterers had gathered round the motor-car. Frau Messinger paid them no attention.

'Will you carry something for me?' she said to me, and pointed at the wet battery of a wireless-set on the floor by the passenger seat. 'Might I ask you to carry it to the garage, and bring the other back?'

It is odd to think that those were the first words I heard her speak. Other boys had previously undertaken this chore: for some particular reason of her own she chose not to drive into Aldritt's garage and have the used battery replaced there by the one that had been recharged. Vaguely, she referred to that when she returned to the motor-car with her shopping, something about it being less of a nuisance like this. She opened the passenger door and showed me how to wedge the battery to prevent it from toppling over. 'I'd really be most awfully lost without the wireless,' she said, giving me a threepenny-piece.

She was an extremely thin, tall woman, her jet-black hair piled high, her eyes blue, her full lips meticulously painted: I had never seen anyone as beautiful, nor heard a voice that made me so deliciously shiver. *You looked for a blemish on her hands, on the skin of her neck or her face*, I wrote in a notebook I kept later in my life. *There wasn't one. I could have closed my eyes and listened to that husky timbre for ever.*

'There is something that hasn't come in to Kickham's,' she said. 'It's due on the bus this afternoon. Might I ask you to bring it out to Cloverhill for me?'

I remember that more distinctly than any other moment in my life. She was already in the car when she spoke, and her tone of voice was not one normally employed when making a request.

4

With a gentle imperiousness, she commanded what she wished, and before she drove away she glanced at me once, a smile flittering across her thin features. The street-corner loiterers watched the slow progress of the car until it was out of sight, and then returned to lean again against the corner of Duggan's public house. I stood where I was, still aware of tremors dancing beneath my skin.

'What kind of a female is she?' my father enquired when he discovered – not from me – that I'd been addressed by Frau Messinger on the street. He was surprised when I told him that in my opinion she was an Englishwoman. He insisted I was mistaken, just as later he refused to accept that the Messingers were not Jews: in times like these, he said, no Englishwoman in her sane mind would marry a Hun, it stood to reason. 'Amn't I right?' he persuaded my mother, and she – not really listening – said he was of course.

We were a Protestant family of the servant class which had come up in the world, my father now the proprietor of the timberyard where he had once been employed. He was a bulky man, inclined to knock things over; he thought of himself as easygoing and wise. My mother's hands were swollen and red from washing clothes and floors and dishes; her greying fair hair was forever slipping out of its hairpins. My two grandmothers, who lived with us, had not addressed one another since my parents' wedding-day. My two brothers, younger than I was, were chunkily built twins, their identities often confused even within the family. My sister Annie – already working in the office of the timberyard – was jealous because I had been sent away to the grammar school at Lisscoe and she had not, and because my brothers would be sent away also. She resented the dullness of the employment she was so often told she was lucky to have. She wanted to work in a shop in Dublin.

Our house was the last building in Laffan Street except for the sheds and concrete stores of the timberyard next door. It was a pale-brown house, of painted stucco, without railings to separate it from the pavement and without steps in front of its hall-door. The windows of its three storeys had net curtains as well as heavier curtains and blinds. The narrow, steep stairway that ascended from the hall to the attics was a central vein, supplying access to trim, short landings on the first and second floors. There was an upstairs sitting-room that was never used, the kitchen and the dining-room forming between them the household's heart. My brothers spread their schoolbooks out on the dining-room table, as Annie and I had once upon a time done also. The kitchen adjoined, with a hatch in the wall for convenience. My grandmothers sat in two armchairs by the dining-room window, watching the people going by on the street; in cold weather they sat on either side of the fire, not looking at one another. When we were small Annie and I used to share a bedroom, but now we had one each: patterned linoleum on the floor, an iron bedstead, wash-stand and cupboard, just like our parents' bedroom and our brothers'.

These rooms, the steep stairway and the landings, the square backyard you could see from the bedroom windows, its red outhouse doors and the sloping roof of its turf shed: all that constituted my familiar childhood world, and the town that lay beyond this territory of home reflected it in many ways, though at the time I did not notice this. It was a scrappy, unimportant little town, a handful of shops and public houses in narrow streets, its central square spoilt by two derelict houses and a statue to a local martyr. Bridge Quay and Bridge Lane ran off Laffan Street: Nagle Street was where Reilly's Café and the two better grocers' shops were, separated by Kickham's drapery. The Wolfe Tone Dance-hall resembled a repository for agricultural implements – a relentless cement façade halfway up Wolfe Tone Hill, with a metal grille drawn across by day, the week's band announced on a bill stuck to a nearby telegraph pole. On the outskirts of the town was the Church of Our Lady, and at the end of St Alnoth Street the slender spindle of the Protestant Church of St Alnoth was dark against the sky.

I walked through the town on the first of my journeys to Cloverhill, clutching a soft, brown-paper parcel from Kickham's. I wondered what it contained and tried to feel beneath the string and the overlap of paper, but was not successful. I felt excited, quickening my stride as I passed the abandoned gasworks and the hospital that was being built, branching to the right at the signpost where the road divided. *Ballinadee* the signpost said, 2½ *miles*. The road became narrow then, and there were no cottages all the way to the white gates of Cloverhill, which were set in a crescent sweep bounded by a stone wall. An avenue meandered through fields where sheep grazed except where the land had been ploughed. From the moment I passed through the gates I could see the house in the distance, in grey, stern stone against treeless landscape.

Astride a farm horse, a man rode towards me. 'You have come with my wife's ordering,' he said. 'You are good to her.' He was a small, square man, too muscular to be described as fat, with short sandy hair and a drooping eyelid. Agreeably, he asked me my name and where I lived. When I told him my father was the proprietor of the timberyard he replied that that was interesting. He himself, he informed me before he passed on, cultivated sugar-beet mainly.

The fields on either side of the avenue became uncared-for lawns, with flower-beds in them. There was a gravel sweep, steps led to a white hall-door. I pulled the bell-chain and heard, a moment later, the tap of the maid's heels on the flagged floor of the hall. At Cloverhill, I discovered later, the Messingers lived with this single servant, a girl of seventeen or eighteen with attractively protruding teeth, called Daphie. Two farm-workers, one of them her father, came by day. In the Messingers' marriage no children had been born.

I was led into the drawing-room, where Frau Messinger was sitting on a green-striped sofa, made comfortable with green-striped cushions bunched into the corner behind her. She was smoking a cigarette. As on all future occasions when I visited her

7

in this room, she wore red, this time a scarlet dress of a soft woollen material, with a black silk scarf knotted loosely at her throat. In other ways, also, it was always just the same: I would enter the elegantly furnished drawing-room and be subjected to wide-eyed, frank appraisal, an examination that was accompanied by a smile. She never said much at first. When the tea was brought she poured it and at once lit a fresh cigarette, then leaned back against her cushions, her eyes not leaving my face, her smile still lingering. Sometimes, for an instant before she settled herself, the black lace hem of her petticoat showed. Then she would tidy her skirt about her knees and the lacy hem would not again be seen.

'This is kindness itself,' she said that first time. 'Boys are not often kind.'

I deprecated her compliment, but was ignored. A silence fell. She guessed my age, and said that she herself was twenty-seven, her husband sixty-two. I did not, at the time, find anything odd in that; I did not think of Frau Messinger as a girl, which is how I remember her now, nor of her husband as an old man, which later he appeared to me to be. All that seemed peculiar to me then was that we just drank tea: there was nothing to eat, not even a sandwich or a biscuit.

'Both of us were born beneath the sign of Sagittarius,' she said. Not that she entirely believed in the astrology notes she read in magazines, yet she could not quite resist them. 'Do *you* like reading just for fun?' she asked and then, not waiting for an answer, described the various German and French magazines that had delighted her when she'd lived in Germany. What she'd enjoyed most of all was drinking afternoon chocolate in a café and leafing through the pages of whatever journals were there. She described a café in a square in Münster where the daily newspapers were attached to mahogany rods that made them easier to read, and where there were magazines on all the tables. Guessing that I had never been in a theatre, she described the orchestra and the applause, the painted scenery, the make-up and the actors. She described a cathedral in Germany, saying she and Herr

Messinger had been married in it. 'Harry, do you think you could save me a horrid journey and bring out the wet battery from Aldritt's on Tuesday?'

This was the indication that my present visit had come to an end. There was the lavish smile, and the assumption that naturally I would agree to carry out the wireless battery. Without hesitation, I said I would.

'I hear you were at Cloverhill,' my father remarked that evening, when all of us were gathered around the dining-table from which we ate our meals. The family atmosphere was as it always was: my grandmothers silent in their dislike of one another, my brothers sniggering, my mother tired, Annie resentful, my father ebullient after an hour or so in the back bar of Viney's hotel.

'Cloverhill?' Annie said, her lips pouting in a spasm of jealousy. 'Were you out at Cloverhill?'

'I had a message from Kickham's.'

'So you'd say they were Jews?' my father said.

I shook my head. Since the Messingers had been married in a cathedral it seemed unlikely that they could be Jewish. He came from a village near a town called Münster, I said; she was definitely English.

'Well, I'd say they were Jews.' My father cut a slice of shop bread with the bread-saw, scattering crumbs from the crust over the table-cloth. 'The Jew-man goes to the synagogue. There's no synagogue in this town.'

My father lent his observations weight through his slow delivery of them, his tone suggesting revelations of import yet to come. But invariably this promise remained unfulfilled.

'I'm surprised you were running messages for them,' my sister said.

I did not reply. I would tell my companions at the Reverend Wauchope's rectory – Mandeville, Houriskey and Mahoney-Byron – about the Messingers: it was clearly no use attempting to convey anything about them to any member of my family. One of my brothers upset a cup of tea, and with a vigour that belied the weariness in her features my mother delivered a slap to the side of his face. The less squat of my grandmothers exclaimed her approval; the other muttered in distaste. The subject of the Messingers did not survive this interruption; my father talked about the war.

On Tuesday I collected the charged battery at Aldritt's garage and carried it out to Cloverhill. It was made of glass, and fitted into a wire cage with a handle: it wasn't difficult to carry, nor was it heavy. Frau Messinger gave me a list that afternoon, and the packets and the single parcel I conveyed to Cloverhill two days later were hardly a burden either. Then it was time to collect from Aldritt's the battery I had myself left there a week before. I even learnt how to connect the wires of the wireless-set to it.

'Harry, I should like to tell you a little about my mother and myself,' Frau Messinger said on the last afternoon of my holidays, a warm afternoon in September when the French windows of her drawing-room were wide open. A bumblebee buzzed intermittently, alighting on one surface after another, silent for a moment before beginning its next flight. The last bumblebee of summer, she said, and added without any change of voice, as though the same subject continued:

'My mother was a poor relation, Harry. From my earliest childhood that was an expression that accompanied us everywhere we went. Often, in Sussex, my mother would wave one of her tiny hands at the landscape and announce that it was the family's. I also distinctly recall her doing so on the sea-front at Bognor Regis, implying with her delicate little wave all the houses of the promenade, and the seashore as well.'

She handed me the stub of her cigarette and asked me to take it to the garden and throw it away, out of sight somewhere, poked down into a flower-bed, she suggested. It was the first time she made this request of me, but she was often to make it in the future: the smell of stale cigarettes was unpleasant in a room, she explained, answering the bewilderment on my face.

'You naturally wonder about my father,' she said when I

returned. 'Who he was and why he was never with us. Well, I'll tell you, Harry: I never knew my father. I never so much as laid an eye on him or heard his voice or even saw a photograph. My father was a dark horse. My mother wore a wedding ring, but I am honestly not sure that she did so with any title. I rather believe my father was something dreadful, like a pantryman.'

I did not know what a pantryman was, nor do I to this day. But I could tell from the lowered voice accompanying the revelation that in Frau Messinger's view a pantryman was a long way down the scale from a butler, or even a footman. Her mother had become enamoured of a lesser servant.

'My mother, no matter what else she was, Harry, was a very foolish little person. If she had not been foolish about some tedious investment she would not have become a poor relation. She was taken in by a solicitor in Sevenoaks who claimed he could make a fortune for her. She was lucky to have ended up with anything at all left. But not enough for my education.'

Her cigarette-lighter was round, like a polished gold coin. Sometimes she played with it while she talked. Sometimes she took a cigarette from her yellow Gold Flake packet, then changed her mind and returned it, tidily folding the silver paper as it had been folded before.

'My mother stayed in people's houses: that's how we lived. We went from house to house, in a circle all over Sussex, and when we arrived at a certain point we began all over again. Governesses taught me, Harry. I was passed from schoolroom to schoolroom in the houses where we stayed, from Miss Kindle to Miss D'Arcy, to Miss Moate, to Miss Hindhassett, on to Miss Binding and Miss Gubbins. To tell the truth, Harry, I'm hardly educated at all. I mean, a smattering. I have nothing more.'

I formed a picture of the existence she described, of arriving with her mother and their luggage in this house or that, endlessly beholden. I saw her as the child she'd been, much taller than her mother, just as she was taller than her husband: a thin, lanky child was what she'd said, not very happy. I knew nothing of the kind of houses she spoke of, and imagined palaces in soft English countryside, with gardeners and parlour maids. She and her mother travelled by train, and someone met them at the railway station. Often it wasn't actually a railway station but a special stopping place in the middle of nowhere, a 'halt', she called it, used only by the people of the nearby estate.

Even now, so very long afterwards, I can clearly see the clothes she described to me: her favourite dress when she was twelve, in forget-me-not blue with tiny white dots that were flowers when you looked closer, and plain white buttons; her favourite dress when she was fifteen, of crimson velvet, the first of her red dresses; the lace stole she was given once; green shoes she'd had. Furniture in the houses she'd visited remained vivid in her recollection, and has passed into mine: a Queen Anne dressing-glass of inlaid rosewood, so delicately finished that she had always had difficulty in drawing her eyes away from it; a gold-faced clock on a mantelpiece in a hall; pale Chippendale chairs around an oval table. On the day after her eighteenth birthday a young man had proposed marriage to her, and she wept because she loved him but even so rejected him. They had walked together through a meadow where poppies bloomed, then by a river and an apple orchard. That year she had learnt Italian. That year she had tried particularly to be good at tennis, which she had always wanted to be. At nineteen she had become religious, and had wondered about the Virgin Mary and the mystery of the Annunciation.

'You will wonder why we were in Germany, Harry. Well, it's the same kind of thing as staying in other people's houses. Mrs Marsh-Hall needed a companion to travel with, her sister having died the previous year. So she took my mother with her as well as a maid, and of course I was permitted to go along. Otherwise I would never have met my husband.'

When she spoke of that time Frau Messinger uttered a few words in German before returning to English to tell me about her husband's many sisters and his cousin who was unable to speak because of a stroke, his niece who'd been a singer and lived with the family in their *Schloss*. Herr Messinger had been left a widower seven or eight years ago; he had three sons in Hitler's army.

'None of it is nice for him, Harry. "You must buy land with the house in Ireland," I said. "You must be occupied." For my husband, idleness is a penance.'

She offered me a cigarette, the first time she had done so. She held out the packet casually, appearing not to consider it unusual that a boy of fifteen should smoke. I accepted it because at the grammar school I often smoked behind the lavatories.

'My mother died, Harry, or else you would have met her. She would have come here with us, I think.'

Her tone was not melancholy. She seemed happy to have only Herr Messinger. People had come to call when she had first arrived at Cloverhill, women mainly, bearing visiting cards to represent their husbands, since husbands tended to be occupied at that time of day.

'Of course I returned the calls, Harry. Well, really, it would be rude not to.'

But social life ended there. There were invitations to bridge and whist parties, but neither Frau Messinger nor her husband had any interest in card-playing.

'Yet of course we were right, Harry, to come to Ireland. We are proved right every day. Adolf Hitler apologised, you know, when a bomb fell out of one of his aeroplanes on to a creamery somewhere – in Co. Tipperary, was it?'

She didn't care for Adolf Hitler, nor did Herr Messinger, eventhough his sons were fighting for the Nazis. She had fallen in love with Germany and almost overnight Germany had become a tragedy.

'Old women sat in the cafés of Münster, Harry, their faces crinkled in despair at what they read in the newspapers and the magazines. And then the horrible Brownshirts would go by, goosestepping with their legs. You couldn't help loving the manners of the Germans, but what good were manners then?'

I held my cigarette as nonchalantly as I could, dangling it as she was dangling hers.

'It's such a disappointment, Harry, that people can be so silly. Don't you think it is?'

She went on talking, not waiting for my response. Herr Messinger could hardly bear even to think about the sadness that had befallen Germany. 'And poor England, too, Harry – those horrid bombs coming out of the darkness!'

The houses she had visited in Sussex were maybe in ruins by now. People lived on a rasher of bacon a month, and eggs made from powder. In England clothing wasn't warm enough. In Germany the elderly died.

'We're creatures of absurdity, you realise, my husband and myself. Creatures of ridicule, Harry, sitting out two countries' conflict.'

It hadn't been easy for her husband to come away, to leave his family behind, his sisters and his sons. When he read the news in the papers he wondered if they still survived.

'They are not permitted to communicate, Harry. We must wait to know until all this is over.'

She would have been arrested and sent to an internment camp in Germany, as Herr Messinger would have been in England. Every indignity that could be devised would have been visited on them. And the one remaining free would have been reviled for marrying the other.

'I am ashamed of my country when I think of that, Harry. As my husband is of his. That the innocent should be ill-treated, even allowed to die, in the glorious name of war: what kind of world have we made for ourselves?'

He had tried to persuade his sisters, and all the household of the *Schloss*, to accompany them to Ireland; his sons would not have been allowed to. But it was easier for his sisters to continue with the familiar than to embark upon the strangeness of a country they had scarcely heard of. And they were getting on in years, and less pessimistic about the future than their brother.

'So we came alone to our sanctuary, and live with the guilt of it, Harry. There is always guilt in running away.'

Listening to her voice, I found myself wondering what happened in the drawing-room after my afternoon visits. Did she lie for a little longer on the sofa and then rise from it to prepare a meal for her husband? It was hard to imagine her with her sleeves rolled up and an apron tied over her dress. She did not appear to belong in a kitchen, with meat and vegetables and bread-soda. Yet Daphie did not strike me as someone capable of preparing meals: Daphie belonged more with brushes and dusters and tins of Brasso. A long time later I discovered that Herr Messinger did all the cooking at Cloverhill.

'Always be gentle with my husband, Harry. Not just his country, but a way of life, has been destroyed by criminals. That is not pleasant for any man to bear, you know.'

She had never before spoken of Herr Messinger in this manner, and certainly I had not thought of him as someone with whom it was necessary to be gentle. Yet now, so long afterwards, I understand, for the pictures that filled his mind – his sons engaged in futile battles, the *Schloss* a barracks, the old women weeping in the cafés – must daily have felt like a canker consuming him.

'When I was young, Harry, far younger than you are now, I used to wonder what life was going to be like.' She smiled in her sudden way, her evenly arranged teeth whitely glistening. She had imagined an existence in the English countryside, watching her mother growing old, collecting bone china. 'I always loved pretty things, Harry. Thimbles and tiny mantelpiece ornaments. Such little objects were always in the houses we stayed at, but of course they were never mine. My husband has made up for that.'

She showed me a cabinet full of *objets d'art* that I had hardly noticed before, in the corner of the drawing-room. Some of the china was German, some English. 'Cheek by jowl, Harry, making the silly war seem sillier.'

In a small garden she would have grown anemones, which

15

were her favourite flower. 'I did not see how I could marry, yet later I did of course.' She smiled but did not explain that further: why it was she had chosen Herr Messinger, having rejected the young Englishman whom I had so very clearly seen walking with her in the poppied meadow on the day after her eighteenth birthday, when there were tears on her cheeks because she was in love. Herr Messinger, with his lined, square face and his drooping eyelid, was different in every way from the dark-haired figure in a white cotton suit and panama hat I had imagined. 'It was impossible that my husband and I should not marry,' was all she said.

I left her reluctantly on the last day of my holidays, wondering who would fetch the glass batteries for her until I returned, hoping no one would. Her eyes smiled her own particular farewell at me as she lay languid on the sofa, a cigarette she had not yet lit between her fingers. The bumblebee was still in the room, darting between the two brass lamps that hung from the ceiling, settling on one glass globe and then the other, before again becoming restless.

As I walked through dwindling sunshine, down the avenue and out on to the empty road, strange fantasies possessed me. I saw with vividness the Messingers' marriage in the German cathedral, candles alight on the altar, guests mysterious in a twilight gloom. I heard the singing of a choir, and then the bridal couple were in their honeymoon bedroom, she still in her wedding-dress, he pouring champagne into glasses. They ate slices of their wedding cake and laughed in their happiness, defying the war that already threatened to deprive them of it.

2

At the Reverend Wauchope's rectory, in the bedroom I shared
with Mandeville and Houriskey and Mahoney-Byron, I journeyed
again to Cloverhill, as I do in my memories to this day. At the
grammar school my inability to learn what I was required to
learn was soothed by possessive daydreams, my failure to make
sense of mathematical abstractions lightened. Although later I
wished I had not, I described to my companions at the rectory
Frau Messinger's flawless skin and the way she had of smiling
when she looked at you, and her jet-black hair. I mentioned her
perfectly painted lips. 'Holy Jesus!' Mandeville whispered, his
voice reverent with envy; Houriskey wanted to know if I ever got
a look up her skirts. At Lisscoe grammar school there was a lot of
talk like that; all humour was soiled, double meanings were
teased out of innocence. When I described the clothes Frau
Messinger wore I could see from Mahoney-Byron's expression
that, one by one, he lifted the garments from her body.

'You haven't a snap of her?' Mandeville asked quietly.

'There are only the wedding photographs in her bedroom.'

'Were you in her bedroom?'

'She showed me one time.'

'Jesus Christ, man!' Houriskey and Mahoney-Byron shouted,
perfectly in unison, but Mandeville's reaction was more intense
and private. Mandeville was an emaciated boy with spectacles,
the ravages of a departed acne still evident about his nose and
chin. He had wavy fair hair that he brushed back from his fore-
head, with a central parting. Mandeville was besotted by the
younger of the two English princesses, an infatuation that had
developed in him the ambition to find employment of some kind

in Buckingham Palace. Houriskey and Mahoney-Byron were bigger, heavier boys, the sons of farmers.

'What'd she show you in the bedroom?' Houriskey asked.

'Nothing; only what it was like. She showed me every room in the house one time.'

'Why'd she do that?'

'Because she's bored, I suppose.'

'God, you bugger!'

It had not occurred to me until that moment that she was bored. 'Harry, would you like to see the house?' she had said, then led the way from room to room, pausing longest in the bedroom she shared with her husband. 'You can lie in bed, Harry, and listen to the birds.' It was a room in which, apart from a trouser-press and the pillow on which he rested his head, there was little trace of Herr Messinger. Her hairbrushes and her scent bottles were arranged among the silver-framed wedding photographs on the dressing-table; her dresses hung in a wardrobe which she opened: a row of her shoes stretched between the two windows, their toes neatly in line; her nightdress, silkily pale-green, lay on the candlewick eiderdown; perfume scented the air.

'If she took you into her bedroom she was on for it,' Houriskey said. He laughed coarsely, at the same time as Mahoney-Byron. Mandeville smiled. Houriskey acquired jokes from an odd-job man on his father's farm and conveyed a stock of them to the school with each new term. They had to do with honeymoon couples, mislaid clothing, and intimacies concerning the odd-job man's wife. Raucous laughter emanated from Mahoney-Byron as each anecdote reached its conclusion, but Mandeville always only smiled.

'What's your man Messinger like?' Mahoney-Byron asked. 'Is he a spy?'

I described Herr Messinger. I said I doubted that he was a spy. Mahoney-Byron, who kept photographs of Hitler and Himmler between the pages of his Hall's Geometry, looked disappointed.

'Mr Churchill's stupidity,' Mahoney-Byron liked to drawl in the mocking accents of Lord Haw-Haw, 'has led his island people to the brink of final destruction. There will not be a city street intact unless this addled old man ceases to feed falsehoods to a weary population.'

The rectory was situated beside the grammar school itself – two unadorned brick buildings in the middle of Lisscoe, which was a town more than twice the size of the one I knew so well but offering a similar provincial ambience. The lower panes of all the ground-floor windows of the school were painted white; in the rectory a smell of damp hung about the bare-board passages and the dining-room. On moist days this dampness penetrated to our bedroom, which was mostly occupied by our four beds and the pitchpine cupboard we kept our clothes in. 'We will pray to God,' the elderly Reverend Wauchope had said the first time he led us into this room – an insistence we were to become familiar with, the words demanding that, irrespective of whatever activity was taking place, those involved in it should fall at once to their knees. In her grimy basement kitchen the clergyman's wife vented a sour disposition on the food she cooked, assisted by a maid called Lottie Belle, whose inordinate stoutness contrasted dramatically with the spare frame of Mr Conron, the assistant master at the grammar school, who lodged at the rectory also. Mr Conron's wasted features were twisted in what appeared to be torment; his eyes were shifty.

While I talked about the Messingers in these surroundings and among these people. I sometimes felt I was relating a dream. The open French windows, the bumblebee and the scent of flowers, Herr Messinger astride his farm horse: all of it seemed so remote as to be outside the realms of existence. And why had they taken to me, awkward youth that I was? 'It's good you come, Harry,' Herr Messinger had said. 'A visitor is nice for her.' Did she miss me, I wondered, as I missed her? Did she remember me when she connected the wires to the battery?

'Did you never think of winking at the woman?' Houriskey

suggested. 'You could be sitting there and give a wink that could be an accident.'

'I don't think she'd like being winked at.'

'God, you bugger!'

The four of us walked slowly around a field where cattle grazed, behind the red-brick rectory. When he'd said Grace in the dining-room that evening the Reverend Wauchope had kept us on our feet to announce the number of RAF planes that had returned from a bombing mission. He always did this when the news was good, permitting us to eat immediately when it was not. 'We will pray to God,' he had commanded, and while the grease congealed on the surface of his wife's mutton soup we sank to our knees, our arms clasped around the backs of our chairs in the manner ordained for dining-room gratitude to the Almighty. Mahoney-Byron's plea for similar Luftwaffe success was kept low.

'Sure, why wouldn't he be a spy?' he persisted in the field, reminding me of my father's refusal to accept that the Messingers were not Jews. It was unlikely that a spy would be married to an Englishwoman, I said, but Mahoney-Byron told me to look for morse-code equipment in a barn, maybe hidden under a load of hay. 'There's a man in Dublin,' he went on, 'with his house built in the shape of a swastika so's a Messerschmitt pilot would know where he was. Have a look in case your man has trees planted in the shape of a swastika. Or fences. Have a gander at the fences.'

We began our second circuit of the field. I could not see how spying might be engaged in from Cloverhill House but I did not say so; nor did I reveal that Herr Messinger had three sons in the Nazi army – for which the war at that time appeared to be going well. Norway and Denmark had capitulated. Holland, Belgium and France had fallen. The Messerschmitts Mahoney-Byron spoke of were clearly inflicting greater damage than radio commentators other than the notorious Lord Haw-Haw admitted: listeners at a distance made allowances for the fear that kept the truth obscure.

'I had a dream last night,' Mandeville murmured, removing his wire-rimmed spectacles and wiping them on the cuff of his jacket. His expression indicated that Cloverhill House and the Messingers were deemed exhausted as a conversational topic, at least for the time being. He coughed softly, which was a way of his. 'I was in a room with the King when she came in with a book in her hand. "What's that you're reading?" he says, only she's shy because of myself. But afterwards she comes up to me and says it's a poetry book. There's nothing she likes better than poetry.'

'Write her a letter,' Houriskey urged. 'She'd like to hear you were dreaming about her.'

'The day will come when I'll be telling her about this place, how I was thinking about her every hour that went by.'

'She'd be interested all right.'

As well as Mandeville's belief that he would find employment in Buckingham Palace, other vocational ambitions were aired from time to time. Houriskey's desire was to emigrate to the northern Canadian fishing grounds, a region for which he had developed an affection that puzzled us. Mahoney-Byron wished to pursue a talent he had for throwing his voice, investing inanimate objects, or creatures not normally so gifted, with speech. He believed he would find employment with Duffy's circus, and had contrived an act in which a number of giraffes engaged one another in conversation. As for myself, all I wanted was not to have to work in the timberyard. I would have readily agreed to become a schoolmaster like Mr Conron, or a post-office clerk or a meal-office clerk. But the timberyard and my father's ubiquitous presence in it, the endless whine of the saws, mud pitched up from the wheels of lorries, the rattle of rain on corrugated iron, the bitter odour of resin: that prospect appalled me, and I knew that what would accompany it within myself was the sullenness that had developed in my sister. 'Forty-one years I've been at it,' my father used to say, appropriately altering the reference as another year passed. He had worked in the yard as a child of ten; his own father had run around the town barefoot, the only Protestant child for twenty-nine miles so ill-clad. I dreaded the day when the hall-door would close behind both of us, when we would walk the few yards together to the timberyard, my sister Annie arriving later because the accounts shed didn't open until nine. Larchwood, beech, ash, oak dressed or left in its sawn condition, mahogany in short supply because of the Emergency: this would replace the dank corridors of the rectory and the white-painted classroom windows. At one o'clock I would return over the same few yards with my father and my sister, and my father would hold forth while we ate boiled bacon or chops. My grandmother would ask him to repeat what all of us had already heard only too well; my brothers would snigger. There'd be semolina with a spoonful of blackberry jam, stewed rhubarb in season; there'd be Jacob's Cream Crackers with butter and Galtee cheese if my father was still hungry. That Jacob's invented the cream cracker was one of my father's greatly favoured mealtime statements.

'I have my little dotey with me here.' Mandeville produced from the back pocket of his trousers a grubby newspaper photograph of the princess. 'Is there a lovelier creature alive?'

We agreed that there wasn't and continued our walk in silence, each of us lost in fantasy. I might become a servant at Cloverhill House; I might keep the flower-beds tidy and the grass cut on the lawns; I might work in the fields with Herr Messinger. I wouldn't mind sitting in the kitchen with the young maid, taking my meals with her, and doing whatever they wanted me to do, growing anemones or lighting the fires every morning.

It snowed, surprisingly, in the autumn of that year. We stood around a coke stove in the hall of the rectory, endeavouring to keep warm, while in his homilies the Reverend Wauchope reminded us that thousands of British soldiers were sheltering under canvas, in temperatures far lower than those we were experiencing. The snow covered the huge hollow in front of the school where the town's dust carts dumped their cinders, the intention being that one day the level would reach that of the surrounding ground and allow for the laying out of a hockey pitch. Unfortunately the dust lorries occasionally committed the error of depositing a load of garbage, which was an attraction for rats and seagulls. At least the snow held in check the foetid odour of decay that normally drifted into the classrooms.

I imagined Frau Messinger suffering from the cold also, a rug drawn over her knees on the sofa in the drawing-room, the fingers that grasped her magazine so numb that she had to rub the life back into them. 'Daphie is good at fires,' she had said, but I guessed that in the big draughty rooms it would be chilly, no matter how vigorously the fires blazed. I imagined her husband in the frost-whitened landscape, felling trees and sawing them into logs. He and one of his men would go about the task in silence, skilfully working the cross-saw. Daphie would appear with a can of tea.

'Whatever's this stupid nonsense?' the Reverend Wauchope tetchily demanded one evening, sending for me specially. 'You're making yourself important, are you, with reports of German spies? That amounts to falsehood, you know.'

A rumour had got going in the grammar school, I endeavoured to explain. It was without foundation; it was simply that a German had come to live near the town I came from.

'Rumours are grapeshot for the enemy. We will pray to God.' I didn't listen to his voice, but imagined instead how astonished the Messingers would be if they could see us. She would laugh her tinkling laugh, her head thrown slightly back. He would shrug his shoulders in his expressive way.

'Stand up, man, stand up.' Renewed crossness interrupted my reflections, for I had remained on my knees longer than I should have. 'Your stupidity is a mockery of the human race. Go from my sight, boy.'

Castigated on one score by the Reverend Wauchope, I was approached on another by the assistant master. He sought me

out when I was alone in a classroom, spoke first of the cold weather, made enquiries about my family, then said:

'There's talk of a certain nature that goes on between yourself
and your friends.'

'What kind of talk's that, Mr Conron?'

'You know what I'm referring to. Involving women.' I shook
my head, instantly denying this.

'Mr Wauchope would not discuss things of that nature with
you on account of he's a clergyman. So it falls to myself.'

'I understand, sir.'

'Mandeville carries a photograph of a woman around with
him. There's a certain type of story Houriskey tells. There's stories you've made up yourself apparently.'

'Which stories are those, Mr Conron?'

He turned his tormented eyes away from me. In one of his
trouser pockets he snapped a piece of chalk in half. His fingers
emerged with one portion lightly held. He looked at it. Still doing
so, he said:

'You have a pretence that you go to a house where there's a
woman.'

'A pretence, Mr Conron?'

'Something you'd make up in your mind, the same as Mandeville with the photograph in his pocket. When you'd talk about a
matter like that it would acquire a reality for you.'

I might have explained that, in fact, the opposite had occurred,
but I did not do so. The assistant master said something I didn't
hear and then referred to carnal temptation, enquiring as to my
familiarity with it. 'Bad thoughts are at the root of carnal temptation. Things you'd pretend about.'

'I understand, sir.'

'It's best to avoid talk that would lead the way to it.'

'I'll take your advice, sir.'

Mr Conron regarded a stain on the boarded floor. In a voice so
low that, again, I could hardly hear it he said:

'Did you ever pretend anything about Mrs Wauchope?'

I imagined, when I repeated this, Houriskey's and Mahoney-Byron's raucous laughter, and the intensity developing in Mandeville's expression. I shook my head. I had never pretended anything about Mrs Wauchope, I said; nor, since I was asked this too, about the maid, Lottie Belle.

The eyes closed, in relief or otherwise I had no way of knowing. 'Avoid anything like that,' Mr Conron advised, and I felt ashamed that I had ever spoken of Frau Messinger in the rectory or the school.

'Well, I'll tell you a queer thing,' my father said when I returned home at the end of that term. 'You'll never guess what I'm going to tell you.'

Ponderous head-wagging took place. I said I couldn't guess.

'There's talk of a picture house for the town. Did you ever hear the beat of that?'

I said I never had. There was money in a picture house, my father went on. Maguire the auctioneer had been going to build one nine years ago only he dropped dead. In the length and breadth of Ireland there wasn't a town of the same population that didn't possess a picture house. Didn't it take a cute old Hun to put his finger on the shame of it?

'D'you mean *he's* going to build it?'

'Sure, we're a disgrace to the world,' my father said.

On Christmas Eve the town was crowded with people who had come in from the country, people you did not usually see on the streets. An old man in rags was playing an accordion, tinker women begged. Public houses were noisy, and as I walked down Laffan Street on my way to the Ballinadee road there was an air all around me of expectation and excitement. Soft misty rain had begun to fall; my clothes were wringing wet by the time I reached Cloverhill House.

'Stand by the fire,' Frau Messinger urged in the drawing-room. 'Oh, Harry, you are foolish! You could catch your death!'

Her husband, wearing riding breeches and gaiters, was

crouched on the floor, poring over a mass of papers he had spread out on the fleur-de-lis pattern of the carpet. He was smoking a thin, black cigar and when he greeted me he confirmed what my father had said: he intended to build a cinema. The papers were the plans for its construction. It was a marriage gift for his wife, he said. She had asked for it specially.

'But, Harry, that site they offer me is not good. Too near the slum part of the town.'

Frau Messinger said hardly anything; she never did in her husband's presence. Instead she smiled with pleasure, delighting in his enthusiasm over the drawings on the carpet. His legs were tucked under him, a stubby finger indicated features of the proposed architecture. In the auditorium the seats would be tiered and there would be a balcony; most important of all, apparently, there would be Western Electric sound.

'On the curtains the pattern will be of butterflies, Harry.'

I did not know much about cinemas. Twice during my years at Lisscoe grammar school the Reverend Wauchope had granted permission for his boarders to attend Hussey's Picture House under the supervision of Mr Conron. We had sat enthralled, watching W. C. Fields and Edna May Oliver, and Charles Laughton in *Mutiny on the Bounty*. There'd been no balcony and no curtains such as Herr Messinger described; in the fourpenny seats gangs of ragged urchins had ceaselessly talked and whistled.

'This is where we've chosen instead, Harry.'

The cinema was to be where the two derelict houses stood in the square. It would transform the square, Herr Messinger promised, with baskets of plants hanging at intervals along the façade. *The Alexandra* announced towering letters on a sketch.

'Well, Harry, what do you think?'

'It's grand.'

'The idea is it should be grand. The box-office like so, stairs whichever side you prefer to mount to the balcony. Two usherettes.'

'Usherettes?'

'We have planned the dress: blue with gold on it, epaulettes to the shoulder.'

He showed me a sketch of a girl in such a uniform, then showed me other details: the mechanism that allowed the seats to fold back when they were not in use, the lighting arrangement that caused the butterfly curtains to change colour, the removable ashtrays. When we had perused all that, he gathered the plans and the sketches into a roll and secured them with a rubber band.

'The town will be the better,' Frau Messinger murmured, so softly that the remark was almost lost. People would delight in the cinema, she went on, her tone becoming a little louder. It would be a centre of life, as a church was. From miles around people would ride in on their bicycles for a few hours of relaxation; they would come in traps and jaunting-cars, and when the Emergency was over they would come in motor-cars.

'And, Harry, there is employment for you,' Herr Messinger interrupted. 'When you have finished at that school of yours.'

I looked astonished. He laughed.

'Why not, heh? Would you object to work for me? You choose instead to spend your lifetime with planks of wood? You have a brother, Harry?'

When I replied that I had two he nodded and went on doing so, one eye invisible behind the drooping lid. Since I had two brothers, he pointed out, there was a double reason why I should not be required in my father's business.

'I would place you in the box-office, Harry, to sell the tickets. Later on maybe to oversee the cleaning. To pay the wages of the usherettes. Soon you would learn, Harry. Soon we would learn together.'

My mother would consider that selling tickets in a cinema was inferior to taking my place in the timberyard. My mother's tongue became sharp in anger: having suffered pain and inconvenience bringing four children into the world she demanded sensibleness in return. My father would be bewildered and con-fused, as he was by any deviation from his own assumptions. 'Errah, get on with you, girl,' he'd said when Annie had wanted to go to Dublin to sell dresses in Arnott's or Switzer's. Wasn't she the luckiest girl in the town to have a decent position waiting for her in the accounts shed, with old Miss McLure ready to retire? My mother had been more forceful: she'd given Annie what she called 'a dressing down', pointing out that shop-work was on a par with being a skivvy, that the rest of the family would not be able to hold their heads above the disgrace of it. For days there'd been the sound of Annie's weeping and her blotched face at mealtimes. And, ever since, the sullenness had been part of her.

'So we are arranged,' Herr Messinger said, with confidence. 'Always, since we married, I have dreamed to make a gift like this. Imagine it, Harry, she married an old tortoise like me!' He laughed and kissed her. She clung to him for a moment, whisper-ing something I could not hear. They laughed together; he lit another cigar. He said:

'She wants it to be nice for everyone. I want it to be nice for her. That is how a gift must be.' He went away with his roll of plans, and after a moment his wife offered me a cigarette. I leaned forward so that the flame of her circular cigarette-lighter might catch the tip of it. The brief touch of her fingers was as cold as marble. She said:

'I could not give him children.' Her smile continued to indulge him after he had left the room. Her own name was Alexandra, which was something I had not known before: even though she had failed him, he was offering her a gift which was to be created as she wished, to bring pleasure to strangers. All he asked was that, it seemed: the fulfilment of a whim in her.

'We can live without anything but love, Harry. Always remem-ber that.'

Daphie brought in the tea, and it was poured. I was made to continue standing by the fire, although my clothes were dry by now and in any case would become damp again on my journey home. All the time, while she talked once more about her past, I thought about the offer that had been made to me. I could feel the cosy claustrophobia of the tiny office of the plans, the window in the glass, hands offering money. For the first time – I think the only time – I hardly listened to the childhood incidents related to me, to the speculations about her unknown father's appearance, the journeying through England and through Germany, and Bach mellifluous on the organ in that candlelit cathedral. There would be green tickets, and red and grey, and I would tear them off singly or in twos and threes; I would dole out pleasure to patrons of all ages.

Before I left that day she asked me to kiss her because it was Christmas Eve. I touched her cheek with my lips, and for a moment she slipped her hand into mine. Christmas would be quiet at Cloverhill, she said: she and her husband would exchange presents, and there were presents for Daphie and the workmen. They would sit together by the fire. 'And I have this for you, Harry.'

She gave me a tie-pin, a slender bar of gold. She'd found it years ago, she said, on one of her early-morning strolls about Münster. She'd seen it gleaming on a paving-stone, where someone had lost it the night before. 'I used to wonder about that person,' she said, 'but I haven't for a long time now. It's time I gave this away.'

She showed me how to pin it into my collar, beneath my tie, but on the way home I took it out in case it should again work itself loose. I have never worn it, fearing its loss, but often I take it from my dressing-table drawer and slip it for a moment into my collar before returning it to safety. Of all I have, it is my most treasured possession.

3

In the New Year, workmen began the demolition of the two empty houses in the square and my brothers and I watched from a distance. Stones and bricks were carried away in lorries, the silver-painted railings that had rusted in front of the two gardens suddenly weren't there any more.

'Oh, the Hun boys don't let the grass grow,' my father said, knocking pepper over a plate of sausages in the dining-room. The timber for the new building was to be supplied from our yard, and for that he was naturally pleased, but he had not yet come to terms with Herr Messinger's decision to supply a town in which he was a stranger with a cinema. Between moments of attention paid to his sausages, he remarked upon the swift determination with which the German had acted. 'And isn't it a surprising thing, the way he'd have got the money out of Germany?'

'Did he send for it?' my mother enquired, without much interest.

'Errah, how could he, for God's sake? Isn't there a war raging over there?'

My mother never seemed offended by such scorn, appearing to accept it as her due, even nodding her agreement with it. But just occasionally, perhaps once or twice a year, her pusillanimity gave way to protest and in the privacy of their bedroom she could be heard spiritedly shouting abuse at my father, calling him uncouth and unclean, bitterly asserting she'd rather share a bed with an animal. His own voice in reply was always so mumbling and low that you couldn't hear properly what he said; but his tone suggested that he didn't deny her accusations, perhaps even promised to do better in the future.

30

'Is it she that has the money, boy? Did the woman ever tell you?'

I shook my head. I said I had obtained no knowledge of the Messingers' financial arrangements, or the source or distribution of their wealth. I was not telling the truth since I knew Frau Messinger to have been a poor relation, and her husband to be a member of a well-to-do family. None of that seemed anyone's business except their own; certainly it was not a tit-bit to be carried into the back bar of Viney's hotel.

'There's money there somewhere,' my father said.

We sat around the dining-room table, all of us eating sausages and fried bread, my grandmothers silently cantankerous with one another, my father airing his views. News he had heard during the day's business was imparted at this hour, anecdotes repeated, deaths and births announced.

'They were saying in Viney's,' he reported now, 'that there's marble on order for the front steps. Did you ever meet the beat of that, marble steps for a picture house!'

'Is it the Connemara marble?' my mother enquired.

'What else would it be? What's the price of Connemara, Annie?'

It was a delusion of my father's that because she kept the timberyard accounts Annie was conversant with the price of any commodity that had to do with the building trade. 'Corrugated, Annie?' he had a way of saying in the dining-room. 'What would I give for a three by six?' Further resentment in Annie would fester then, her face becoming even heavier in her resistance to all that was being foisted on her. 'Ah, sure, she's settled in well to the accounts,' I had heard him telling a man on the street one day. 'Sure, what more could she want?'

'When they have the picture house built,' one of my brothers asked, 'will they charge much to go in there?'

My mother told him not to speak with his mouth full of bread because no one could hear him properly. My father, to whom the same objection might have been put, said:

'I'd say they would. I'd say your man would need a big return on his money. What would he charge, Annie, to make sense of the thing?'

My sister said she had no idea. Briefly, she closed her eyes, endeavouring to dispose of my father and the ability she had ages ago been invested with as regards swift calculation. My father did not pursue the matter. Completing the consumption of another sausage, he turned to me.

'Did you ever find out are they Jews?'

'She's a Protestant. They were married in a Catholic cathedral.'

'I'd say you had it wrong.'

At that time of my life, harshly judging my father's opinions and statements, his dress, his clumsiness, his paucity of style, his manner of lighting a cigarette, I found it perhaps more difficult than I might have to forgive him for dismissing the answers I offered to his questions. In retrospect, of course, forgiveness is easier.

'That man's not rough enough to be a Catholic,' my mother put in.

The squatter of my two grandmothers asked us what we were talking about. In a raised voice my father replied that the man out at Cloverhill was going to build a new picture house for the town. 'I've nothing against a Jew-man,' he said. 'He has a head for business.'

'Isn't Colonel Hardwicke out at Cloverhill?' my grandmother asked. 'Running after the maids there?'

'Colonel Hardwicke's dead,' my father shouted, and my other grandmother nodded disdainfully. 'Dead as a doornail,' said my father.

My mother cut more bread. She poured tea into my father's cup. 'There's a picture they're after making in America that's four hours long,' he said. 'Did you hear about that one, Annie?'

'*Gone with the Wind*.'

'What's that, girl?'

'The name of the film is *Gone with the Wind*.'

'It was young Gerrity was telling me when he came into the yard. I'd say it was called something else.'

'*Gone with the Wind* is the only picture that's as long as that. It's coming to the Savoy in Dublin. There's people going up to see it.'

'Cripes!' one of my brothers exclaimed with enthusiasm. 'Wouldn't it be great to be in the pictures for four hours!'

Sharply, my mother told him not to say 'Cripes' in the dining-room. She reminded him that she'd given a warning in this respect before. My brothers were getting rougher with every day that went by, she said, glaring at both of them.

'Mr Wauchope'll knock it out of them.' My father confidently wagged his head, at the same time turning it in my direction. He winked at me. 'What's that big stick you were telling me about, that Mr Wauchope has in a cupboard?'

I looked at him dumbly, extreme denseness in my eyes. 'What stick's that?'

'Hasn't he a blackthorn for beating the living daylights out of any young fellow who'd misbehave himself?' He released a guffaw, winking at me a second time.

'He has a rod for closing the windows with. You can't reach the top part of the windows,' I explained to my brothers, 'so old Wauchope has to hook the end of a rod into them.'

'Is it Mr Conron I'm thinking of in that case?' my father persevered, his hand held up to disguise further winking from my brothers. One of my grandmothers asked him what the matter was, but he didn't answer her. 'Is it Mr Conron that lays into you with the blackthorn?'

'Conron wouldn't have the strength to hit anyone.' I paused, leisurely dividing a piece of fried bread into triangular segments. I imagined myself in the box-office, telling people who asked me that *Gone with the Wind* wouldn't end till one o'clock in the morning. 'Conron's a type of loony,' I told my brothers.

My father was taken aback. The grin that had been twitching about his lips gradually evaporated. Before I'd been sent to lodge in the rectory he used to read from a letter he'd received from the Reverend Wauchope which itemised the attractions of the boarding arrangements for Lisscoe grammar school. Around this same dining-table we had listened to elaborate inaccuracies about well-heated rooms and plentiful supplies of fresh vegetables from the rectory's own garden. The assistant master lodged at the rectory also, the letter said, so that discipline was maintained.

'That's the stupidest thing I ever heard in my life,' my father muttered crossly.

'A boy from Enniscorthy says Conron was in the loony place they have there. He used to roll a hoop along the road. He thought he was Galloping O'Hogan.'

'That's eejity talk, boy. Don't take any notice of it,' my father sternly advised my brothers.

'I'm only saying what I was told,' I said. 'You'd be sorry for poor Conron.'

'What's the trouble?' one of my grandmothers demanded, and I began to repeat all over again what I'd just told my brothers, but my father interrupted me and shouted at my grandmother not to waste her energy listening. 'No man could teach in a classroom if he was a lunatic. We've heard enough of it,' he said to me. 'Annie, did the pine come in?'

There was a film Houriskey had seen in which the main actor was employed in the box-office of a theatre when all the time he wanted to be on the stage. To make matters worse, he fell in love with an actress who passed by the box-office every night. That was the kind of thing you'd have to be careful about. You could become so familiar with a film actress on the screen that before you knew where you were you'd be in love with her, suffering like the actor, or poor Mandeville over the royal princess.

'What's this?' my mother demanded, two days after my slandering of the assistant master. She held in the palm of her hand Frau Messinger's Christmas present. I had hidden it under the drawer-paper in my bedroom.

'It's a tie-pin. You put it in your collar.'

'Where d'you get it?'

'I found it on the street.'

'That's a lie.'

'I found it outside Kickham's on Christmas Eve.'

'That isn't true.'

Tears pressed against my eyelids. I didn't know why they had come so suddenly, or why so urgently they demanded to be released. I realise now they were tears of anger.

'Why are you telling me lies?'

'They're not lies. Someone dropped the thing on the street.'

'Don't tell me lies on a Sunday, Harry. Did you steal it? Did you take it off someone at school?'

'I'm telling you I didn't.'

She stood there in her Sunday clothes, two patches of scarlet spreading on her cheeks, the way they always did when she was cross. I had entered the bedroom I'd once shared with Annie and now had for myself. She'd been there, with the drawer still open. What right had she to go looking in my drawers?

'Frau Messinger gave it to me at Christmas.'

'*Mrs Messinger?*'

'Out at Cloverhill –'

'I know where the woman lives. Are you telling me the truth now?'

'Yes.'

'What'd she give you a Christmas present for?'

'She just gave it to me.'

'She gives you cigarettes too. You come back smelling of cigarettes.'

'I smoke the odd one.'

'If your father heard this he'd take the belt to you.'

I did not reply, and it was my mother who wept, not I. In her navy-blue Sunday clothes she soundlessly wept and I watched the tears come from her eyes and run into the powder of the face she had prepared for going to church. Like Annie and like myself, she was tired of this house, of the two deaf old women who would not civilly address one another, of my father's lugubrious conversation, and my brothers' sniggering. I know that now, but at the time I had no pity for my mother's tears, and no compassion for her trapped existence. I wanted to hurt her because a secret I valued had been dirtied by her probing.

'You will give it back,' she commanded, her voice controlled, her tears wiped away with the tips of her fingers. 'You will give it back to the woman.'

'Why would I?'

'Because I'm telling you to. Because I'm ashamed of you, Harry, as you should be yourself.'

'I haven't done anything.'

'A woman that's not related to a young boy doesn't give him a present. I'm ashamed you would have taken it.'

'There's no harm in a tie-pin.'

My mother hit me. She slapped me across the face, the way she used to when I was younger than my brothers. A sting of pain lingered on the side of my cheek; my whole face tingled hotly.

'You'll give that back to her.'

I blinked, determined not to cry, looking away from her. The tie-pin was a present, I repeated. You couldn't give back a present.

'You'll give it back and you'll have done with going out to that house.' My mother went on talking, fast and angrily, calling Frau Messinger a wanton and a strumpet. 'Oh, a great time she has for herself, with young boys coming out to visit her. Amn't I the queer fool not to have known?'

I remained silent. I had no intention of returning the tie-pin, nor did I intend to discontinue my visits to Cloverhill. If my father knew about this, my mother said, he'd go out there himself and abuse the pair of them.

That wasn't true. My father would never have gone out to Cloverhill House in such a frame of mind, any more than he would have thrashed me with his belt. All during our childhood there had been this threat of my father's violence, but whenever some misdemeanour was reported to him he'd been bewildered and at a loss for words. He had taken no action whatsoever.

'Get ready for church,' my mother said.

Later, as we walked up through the town – my father and my brothers, Annie with my grandmothers – my mother said to me that none of them must know what had occurred, or hear anything whatsoever about the tie-pin. It would upset my brothers and sister, and worry my grandmothers; my father would be beside himself for a month. 'You'll be ashamed when you think about it in church,' she said.

I stared stonily ahead, at my father's back. On Sundays he wore a blue serge suit with a waistcoat, and a collar and tie, and an overcoat when it was cold. It was the only day of the week he looked like a Protestant, a respectable timberyard proprietor who had made his way up in the world, who carried coins in his pocket to distribute among us at the church gates. On other days he wore working clothes, since only they were suitable for the dust and grime of the yard. He still loaded timber himself, and worked the saws and planes. Occasionally he drove one of the lorries.

On the way to church he greeted people he knew among the Catholics coming back from late Mass, the women grasping their prayerbooks, men with collars and ties. You could tell at a glance they were different from us: they didn't often walk in a family as we did, but in ones and twos, with occasionally a huge bunch of children on their own, sprawled all over the street, chattering busily. The children eyed us, but because of my father and mother they didn't shout 'Proddy-woddy-green-guts' or 'dolled-up-heathens'. Our pace was slow because of the two old women, and we always had to leave the house early in order to allow for this. In the church it took them ages to sit down, fumbling and making certain they were as far away from one another as possible. Neither of them stood up for the psalm or the hymns, only for the Creed.

On that particular Sunday, while we progressed through the town and stood waiting in the aisle for my grandmothers to settle themselves, and later while my brothers fidgeted and poked at one another during the service, I continued to be aware of the impression of my mother's hand on the side of my face. I was not a child, I thought, to be struck so; I could not imagine Houriskey or Mahoney-Byron, or even Mandeville, undergoing such humiliation. And again I thought: what right had she to go searching under my drawer-paper?

I listened to my father mumbling the responses and wondered if she hit him in anger also; was a blow ever struck when they had their bedroom disagreements? I doubted it: her sharp tongue would do the work for her, it was children who were hit. Hundreds of times during my childhood I had planned to run away after receiving such punishment; here in this pew, not listening to the pulpit admonitions, I had seen myself arriving in a harbour town and slipping under a pile of canvas on a deck. They would be sorry then. I would be carried away, and white-faced and grief-stricken they would pray for my return.

'You'll go out with it this afternoon,' my mother said on the walk home from church. 'And that'll be the end of the matter.'

She would find it no matter where I put it; not trusting me, she would search high and low. So I hid it at Cloverhill. I dropped it down a crevice between the hall-door steps, and then I pulled the bell-chain. I was shown into the drawing-room and soon afterwards tea was brought in by Daphie. I smoked three cigarettes.

That spring, at school, I received my first letter from Frau Messinger. Her handwriting was neat and sloping, slender loops on the letters that demanded them, dots and cross-strokes where they belonged. *It is such excitement, Harry! We drive in every day. I had not known that building anything could be so much fun.* Steel reinforcements were bathed in concrete, walls rose, rubble was levelled and floors laid down, rain fell on the workmen, the roof went on. *It has brought such joy to my husband, Harry, that so many people should come and stand by him and are pleased at what is happening. But, oh, how I long for it all to be finished, to sit and watch the screen! 'Will the war be over first, or your picture house complete?' a man said to my husband the other day. Once upon a time people were slow to mention the war to him, he being a German, but now all that has gone.*

I still have all her letters of that time, and when I read them now, as often I do, I believe I see Cloverhill as she had come to see it, and the town as she saw it also. In retrospect it is as easy to pass with her from room to room at Cloverhill as it is to keep company with the lanky child who visited the country houses of Sussex in the company of her diminutive mother, or the girl who met in Münster the old man she was to love. She told me once that all her life she had never slept well and as a child had always risen earlier than the servants in those well-servanted households, to explore places she did not have the courage to explore by day. Clearly, I see her. Her solitary figure wanders the morning streets of Münster. She is the first customer in a café; she reaches down a newspaper from its rack. I watch her unlocking the big hall-door of Cloverhill; I watch her descending the three steps on to the gravel sweep, the lawns on either side of it glistening with frost. *Harry will come today*: I have wondered, too, if that anticipation ever flickered in her mind as she strolled among the flower-beds, different in each season. *A boy from the town*: did she write that down in a letter to someone she once knew? Any boy would have done, or any girl: I don't delude myself. Yet so very poignantly I remember her kiss that Christmas Eve, and feel the coldness of the tie-pin passed into my hand. Once I gave her a present myself: two packets of American cigarettes. I bought them from a boy at the grammar school who used to sell such things, cigarettes having become excessively hard to obtain. 'Oh, Harry *darling*,' she said.

Often I am affected by memories of the Messingers together, memories that are theirs, not mine, as if the thrall they held me in has bequeathed such a legacy. Opposite one another at their teak dining-table, they seem quite dramatically an old man and a girl, he entertaining her with an account of the work there has been on the farm that day, her turn now to listen. In their bedroom, they undress and fold their clothes away, the summer twilight not yet night. In their breakfast-room he opens letters while they drink black coffee. Logs blaze and crackle; the sun warms the conservatory that opens off the room. There is music on their wireless.

Later, wrapped up against the weather, they move through the void of the building they have talked about, their footsteps echoing. For the interior walls they choose the shades of amber that later became familiar to me, darker at the bottom, lightening to dusty paleness as the colour spreads over the ceiling. These walls must be roughly textured, they decree, the concave ceiling less so, the difference subtly introduced. Four sets of glass swing-doors catch a reflection of the marble steps that so astonished my father: the doors between the foyer and the auditorium are of the warm mahogany supplied by our timberyard. Long before the building is ready for it, they choose the blue-patterned carpet of the balcony, and the scarlet cinema-seats.

Herr Messinger drives the gas-powered car back to Cloverhill; she leans a little tiredly on his arm as together they enter the house. In the town they have bought things for their lunch. 'We often have just a tin of sardines. Meals should be picnics, don't you think, Harry?'

Time passed. At school the same jokes continued. In the Reverend Wauchope's rectory fat Lottie Belle waddled the same plates of unpleasant food from the kitchen to the discoloured oilcloth spread over the dining-table. At home my father's conversation was changelessly pursued. 'We like this friendship we have made,' Frau Messinger said in her drawing-room.

One April day, when I returned from Lisscoe more than a year after work had first begun on the cinema, I sensed that something was wrong. The building appeared to have reached a standstill. I did not question my father or Annie about this, as I might have done, but instead, continuing to ignore my mother's strictures, walked out to Cloverhill. 'She's sick,' Daphie said, opening the white hall-door to me. 'She's taken to her bed.'

There was no sign of Herr Messinger in the fields or on the avenue and when I returned a week later, to be met by the same response, he was not in evidence either. Nor, to my surprise, did he once appear in the square, though he had regularly done so in the past. Frau Messinger's last letter had not mentioned illness, but had referred as usual to their visiting the building works together. In my frustration I became depressed, was chided by my father for being down-in-the-mouth and made to shovel sawdust in the timberyard, which he said would cheer me up. Then, on the day before I was to return to school, I heard Herr Messinger's voice as I passed his half-completed building. 'But *always* I wait,' he was protesting disconsolately. 'Always I say make haste and always you promise. You are letting me down when I cannot come in every day.'

The builder, a companion of my father's in the back bar of Viney's, began his reassurances. He was doing his best in every hour God sent him; the only trouble was there was an emergency in the country. Materials could not be obtained in the usual manner or at the usual speed. If he'd been asked to construct a cinema five years ago the entire population of the neighbourhood would have been watching Mickey Mouse within a six-month.

'This is moving from the point, though. Since I haven't been able to visit the site your men have slowed down, heh?'

'There's no better men in the land, sir.'

'If they could just be a little swifter on their feet, maybe?'

Turning away for a moment, perhaps to hide his exasperation, Herr Messinger saw me standing there. He nodded, but didn't smile or address me. I'd never known him so uncommunicative.

'I'll tell you what, sir.' Thoughtfully the builder passed a hand over the stubble of his jaw. 'Come back on Thursday and you won't know the place.'

He was a bigger man than Mr Messinger and having completed the massage of his jaw he placed the same hand on the German's shoulder, bending a little to do so. A smile of satisfaction rippled the ham-like complacency of his features. 'I had to pacify the old Hun,' I imagined him saying to my father in the back bar. 'Sure, haven't the poor men only the one pair of legs to each of them?' My father would be duly sympathetic: in the dining-room he had often related how he had similarly extricated himself from the complaints of a customer about a delay due to some oversight in the timberyard.

Herr Messinger said he would return before Thursday; he would return tomorrow; not a day would pass from now on without a visit from him at the building site. In a way that reminded me of my father also, the builder said he'd be welcome. Wasn't it the man who pays the piper that calls the tune? he amiably remarked. When he'd ambled off Herr Messinger spoke to me.

'Well, Harry, so you are back again?'

'Yes.'

'Harry, she is not well. The early months she hates before spring comes. Well, that is wrong, so she says: it is the early months that don't like her. January, February, March too. And this year she was determined to watch the building. So the months took their revenge, Harry.'

'Is she getting better?'

'When you return for the summer you will see for yourself.' He smiled at me; gold glistened in his teeth. 'Oh, Harry, these labourers do not advance much. And then of course it is true: commodities are hard to come by in the Emergency. The architect does not arrive because he has no petrol, and I myself – well, I like to be with her when she is not all right.'

'Please thank her for her letters.'

'When you go back to your school she will write a few more. As she improves, so summer comes again.'

'I'd write back only it's hard to get stamps where I am.'

'Don't worry about writing back.'

'She never said she was ill.'

'That wouldn't be her way, Harry.'

He strode away, dapper in his German clothes, the shine of his gaiters catching the sunlight. Later that morning, in Nagle Street, he waved to me from his car. I wished he'd said that I might visit her in her bedroom. I had thought he might say that: it would be ages now before I saw her.

For her sake I welcomed the mild weather of spring that year, and the warmth of early summer. During the dragging weeks of June there was a heatwave. Was it in June that anemones came? I had no idea.

'You will remember for ever your days in the rectory,' the Reverend Wauchope finally predicted, which were the words of his parting to all the pupils who boarded there. He was, of course, right. 'We will pray to God,' he said, and together he and I did so, he speaking for me, requesting guidance and the blessing of humility in the days of my future. 'I am to understand that you have failed to find affinity with scholarship,' he remarked. 'Nor have you otherwise achieved distinction. Your father is a draper, is he?'

'He has a timberyard, sir.'

'And a place for yourself in it? You are most fortunate. More fortunate than most.'

I did not reply. *After we have died*, the first letter I received during that term had asked, *do you believe there will be a heaven*? Subsequent letters referred to the possibility of this future also; the past, always previously her subject, was not touched upon. Nor was the present: for all the mention there was of it, the building of the cinema might have been defeated by the builder's lassitude and the shortages of the Emergency. The more I searched the lines of the letters for any hint of progress the more I experienced bleak dismay. Instead, repeated often, Frau Messinger had written: *I have never understood how it is we shall be separated, some of us for heaven, some for hell.*

'I have asked you a question,' the Reverend Wauchope said.

'I'm sorry, sir.'

'Do you intend to honour me with an answer?'

'I did not hear the question, sir.'

Only three letters had come; all had to do with life after death.

A week ago the last one had arrived, urging a visit from me as soon as I returned. *The sweet-pea will be in flower and we might walk in the garden.*

'You appear to be inane,' the Reverend Wauchope said. His dry, scratchy voice querulously dismissed me without my having said – as I think I had intended to – that the timberyard did not attract me. But the silence surrounding the Alexandra cinema made me apprehensive about continuing to consider it an alternative. Already I had convinced myself that it had been abandoned because of the illness that was not mentioned. Herr Messinger had lost heart in his gift.

'You are suitable for work with timber,' was the clergyman's final insult, the last thing he ever said to me.

With my three companions of the rectory I walked around the field where the cows grazed, Mandeville confessing that he'd been offered a position in a seed firm, Houriskey and Mahoney-Byron that they'd be going on to their fathers' farms. 'Oh yes, the timberyard,' I said. Mandeville wondered if we'd ever meet again: we thought we probably wouldn't.

Later, in an empty classroom of the school, I gathered together the dog-eared textbooks that had also been my companions for so long and returned them to Mr Conron. Staring hard at some point of interest on the floor, he warned me to be careful in Dublin if one day I should visit it. 'Take care with the women of the quays. Don't be tempted by quayside women.' With these words he offered an explanation for the torment that haunted his features. He lived with shame, yet some part of him was obliged surreptitiously to display its source, half proud confession, half punishment of himself. 'I'll take care all right,' I promised.

I tipped Lottie Belle the two shillings the Reverend Wauchope laid down as a suitable sum for all his boarders to pass on to her, the accumulation of such amounts reputed to constitute the major part of her wages. Mrs Wauchope, who had not addressed me during my years in the rectory, did not do so now.

On a morning in the middle of that same June heatwave I

left Lisscoe for ever. The bus halted to drop off bundles of news-papers or to pick up the passengers who stood waiting at a crossroads or outside wayside public houses, or nowhere in par-ticular. Towns passed through were similar to my own or just a little larger. Cattle drowsed in the fields, familiar landmarks slipped by. The bus was dusty and hot, its air pungent with the fumes of petrol; once it stopped because a woman was feeling sick. I wondered if I would ever make a journey anywhere again, if I was seeing for the last time the ruins by the river, the bunga-low embedded with seaside shells, the green advertisement for Raleigh bicycles on the gable-end of a house: my father boasted that he was none the worse for having never in his life been on a bus. *We live and then we are forgotten*, she had written. *Surely that cannot be the end of us?* In the bus I re-read the three letters I had most recently received, phrases and paragraphs already known to me by heart. *A gravestone gathers lichen, flowers rot in the grave-vase.* In her drawing-room I could not recall her having once even touched upon this subject. She had not, for instance, speculated on the after-life of her dead mother, even though it was apparent from all she said that she had been more than ordinarily fond of her. She had not, when deploring the deaths of so many young soldiers in the war, ever wondered if that was truly the end of them.

The bus drew up by the martyr's statue in the square, taking me unawares because the melancholy nature of my thoughts still absorbed me. The bus conductor handed down my single, heavy suitcase from the luggage rack on the roof, and then I was aware of the reddish tinge of a building that made the square seem dif-ferent. In bright sunlight I gazed at a façade that was exactly as it had been on the architect's sketch, the baskets of flowers hanging from a hugely jutting ledge that formed a roof above the marble steps. *The Alexandra* proclaimed stylish blue letters, as if her hand had written them across the concrete.

4

The flush in her cheeks was like the pink that may creep into the petals of a rose that should be purely white. She lay on her sofa, exactly as she had in the past, smoking and dispensing tea. It was a Sunday afternoon.

'I think you understand everything now, Harry?'

I shook my head but today she did not, as in the past, ignore my responses in our conversation. She observed my gesture, and smiled a little. She said:

'Everything here, Harry? All there has been at Cloverhill?'

'No,' I said.

'The cinema will open in a fortnight. With *Rebecca*. Harry, do you know *Rebecca*?'

She spoke lightly and with her usual casualness, but already I knew that death was everywhere in the drawing-room, and when I walked with her in the garden it was present also. The sweet-pea blooms were a trellis of colour – a dozen shades of purple and mauve, reds lightening and deepening, pinks and whites. Yellow hung from the laburnum shrubs, scarlet dotted the rose bushes. Yet the beauty of the Englishwoman chilled the blaze. Like a ghost sensed coldly, the melancholy of time deserting her was everywhere in the garden, as it had been in the drawing-room.

'Sweet-pea is my second favourite,' she said, and I could tell she knew that at last my density had been penetrated. 'Sweet-pea in a cut-glass vase, set off by the fern of asparagus.'

We walked slowly among the flower-beds. Occasionally she bent down to pull out a weed. Mignonette was her third favourite, she said, but only because of its fragrance.

'I knew nothing about a garden when first we came to Cloverhill,' she said. 'He rescued it for me, you know.'

Brambles had flourished among the rhododendrons and the blue hydrangeas then, cornus was rampant. Fuchsia roots and bamboos had spread beneath the earth, escallonia was smothered. Her husband had dug the flower-beds out; he had discovered lost japonica, he had teased the straggles of jasmine back to health.

'I helped of course, Harry, but sometimes the work was heavy. And there was the farm as well.'

All that had been happening at the time of my first visits to Cloverhill. 'Look at that,' Herr Messinger had said once, showing me his hands, begrimed and scratched, nails broken, the pigment of vegetation colouring his palms. And often from the drawing-room window I had seen him dragging from the garden a cart loaded high with the undergrowth he had cut out. I had hardly noticed, I had not been interested; I had passed through the bedraggled garden without respecting its slow recovery.

'It would be nice to have that time again, Harry, I often think. To go back to the first day we arrived at Cloverhill, waiting in the emptiness for our furniture. We walked about the garden and through the fields. "There is a world to do," he said, and in my happiness I embraced him because I knew he loved to do things. It would be nice to experience again the afternoon you first came here, when Daphie said to me, "There is a visitor." How shy you were, Harry! You hardly said a thing.'

Our progress had slowed down. She took my arm to lean on. We crossed the gravel sweep and went around the side of the house, finally reaching the lawn on to which the drawing-room French windows opened.

'That may be what heaven is, Harry: dreaming through times that have been. Tea in the drawing-room, and how you listened to my silly life!'

We stepped through the French windows, but she did not move towards the sofa. Instead she held her cheek out for me to kiss, and said when I had done so:

'If heaven is there, Harry.'

I was alone then in the room, and some intuition insisted that I had been with her for the last time, and for the last time had heard her voice. And yet as soon as these thoughts occurred I denied them, for how on earth could I know anything of the kind?

As I made my way down the avenue, Herr Messinger called to me from a field, where he was forking hay with one of his men. I clambered over the white-painted iron railing and crossed to where they worked. He came to meet me as I approached.

'Are you finished now at school, Harry?'

'Yes, I am finished now.'

'Well, that is good. You will work for me when the cinema is ready, heh? A fortnight, Harry.'

'Yes, I will work for you.'

'It has taken so long. How often I lost heart!'

I tried to say I was glad he hadn't, because I knew that without his energy and his determination the cinema would still be only half-built. I stumbled in my speech, finding the sentiments difficult to express.

'Ah, well, Harry.' He shook his head and turned away. She had been given a cinema because in such circumstances the giving of a gift had to be as great. And naturally he had wanted it to be swiftly completed. 'Herr Messinger,' I called after him, which was something I would have been too shy to do in the past. 'Herr Messinger, would you like me to assist you with the hay?'

He nodded very slightly, not turning to face me, and so I remained, working in silence beside him and his employee. When twilight came, and darkened, we did not cease because there was mown hay still lying. At home they would wonder where I was, and would be angry. All unusual behaviour made them angry. But as the moon rose and we piled up the last of the haycocks I didn't care about any of that.

'Come back to the house, Harry,' Herr Messinger said when he had finished. 'You are surely hungry.'

So I accompanied him on the avenue and around to the back

of the house, across a yard I had never seen before, and into the kitchen. He lit a lamp because there was no electricity at Cloverhill. He placed it in the centre of the scrubbed wooden table.

'She'll have gone to bed,' he said. 'We're on our own, Harry.'

His workman had ridden off on a bicycle, and I thought it honourable the way Herr Messinger had thanked him so genuinely for working on a Sunday and had said there would be something extra in his wages. In the kitchen he said it was Daphie's evening off. There was a potato salad already prepared, he said, and cold meats with lettuce and tomatoes. He hoped that would be sufficient for us. And wine, he remembered, not very good wine, but he had a little in the larder. 'The chromium for the foyer is to arrive tomorrow,' Herr Messinger said. 'And all the seating at the end of the week.'

We ate cold chicken and pork, and the salad. The wine was the colour of very pale straw, the first wine I had ever tasted; I thought it delicious. 'Ever since I knew her, Harry,' Herr Messinger suddenly said.

His square, hard face was solemn, though there were still crinkles of what I'd always taken to be amusement around his eyes. She would be asleep already, he said; she could not manage food in the evenings. He took tiny amounts on his fork, lifting the fork slowly to his mouth and then replacing it for a moment on his plate, sipping his wine.

'An old man marries for the time that is left, Harry. Both of us seemed not to have much time. Well, there you are.'

I was not hungry; I did not any longer want the pale-straw wine. But he, of course, was used to things being as they were, and ate and drank as usual. I had no knowledge of death: I had never experienced its sorrow or its untimely shock. 'Well, that was sudden,' my father would say before sitting down in the dining-room, and then reveal the name of a person who had died. 'God's mercy,' the Reverend Wauchope's scratchy voice would plead in the prayers to do with losses in the war. Shops closed their doors when a funeral crept by, the blinds of windows drawn down to honour the flower-laden coffin, the hooves of black-plumed horses the only sound.

Herr Messinger lit one of his small cigars. In silence he made coffee. I lifted from the table the plates off which we had eaten and placed them on the draining-board by the sink. I ran the tap but he said that Daphie would attend to all that when she returned. He spoke again of his wife.

'She will see the cinema open its doors. I know that in my heart and she in hers. She will taste the promise of its nights of pleasure. It worried her that we would only come and go at Cloverhill.'

He handed me my coffee, and pushed the sugar nearer. I saw the tears on her cheeks in the moment when she realised she must not marry the young man who had taken her to the poppy field. Had that broken her heart? I wondered.

'You must not worry yourself, Harry.'

'I'm only sorry.'

'The last months would have been empty if there had not been the building. Emptiness is the enemy.'

Soon after that I left. The night was warm, the moon a clear disc, untroubled by clouds. I had never before seen Cloverhill at night, and when I stopped to look back at the house I did not want to turn my gaze away. A pale sheen lightened the familiar grey façade and, in a way that seemed almost artificial, related trees and stone. Blankly, the dark windows returned my stare, a sightless pattern, elegant in the gloom. Did she suffer pain? I wondered.

'Where d'you get to, boy?' my father enquired, calling out to me from the dining-room. 'What time of the night is this to be coming in?'

I stood in the doorway. I could hear my mother rattling dishes in the kitchen, and a moment later she entered the dining-room with a tray of cups and saucers for the breakfast. My father was slouched in one of the old rexine-covered chairs by the fire-place, his slippered feet resting on the grate. Newspaper and kindling would remain unlit in the grate until October, when this positioning of my father's feet would not be possible. Sometimes he forgot and scorched his slippers.

'Your mother's beside herself, boy. Were you drinking or what?'

'Frau Messinger's dying,' I said, but neither of them responded. My food had been ready at half-past six, my mother said; every day, Sundays included, that was the time. She wasn't a maid in her own house, she said: she wasn't a servant. 'Half-six,' my father repeated. 'If you want your grub half-six is the hour, boy.'

My mother took the saucers singly from the pile on her tray, and placed on each an inverted cup. She took cork mats from a drawer in the sideboard and laid the table with knives and forks and side plates. She didn't say anything, but listened while my father repeated what had been established already. He informed me that a meal had been fried for me and had sat in the oven until it was burnt. A waste of food that had already been paid for, he said, and hadn't my mother more to do than pander to the comings and goings of a youth? He reminded me it was a Sunday, the day of the week when my mother might be given an easy time. With painful deliberation he pressed open a packet of ten Sweet Afton and withdrew a cigarette, appearing to select one. 'Where were you drinking?' he said.

'I wasn't drinking.'

'You have drink taken, boy. You brought a smell of it into the house.'

'I had a glass of wine.'

My father scraped a match along the sandpaper of a matchbox. He examined the flame before raising it to his cigarette.

'Wine?'

'Yes.'

'You were out with those people,' my mother said.

'Where're you going now for yourself?' my father demanded, noticing that I had made a move.

'Up to bed.'

51

'Will you listen to that! As cool as water and the whole house after being in a turmoil!'

'You gave me a promise you wouldn't go out there.' My mother had suddenly become still. With a fork in her hand, her eyes hotly probed mine.

'I didn't promise anything,' I said.

I could see her deciding to cross the room to hit me, then deciding against it. My father said I'd had a good education, that money he couldn't spare had been spent on me. 'That food was taken out of the oven at twenty past eight,' he said. 'There isn't a dog in the town would have thanked you for it.'

'You promised me that day.' My mother did not take her eyes off me; I thought she hated me because I could feel something like hatred coming across the room from her.

'I nearly went down to the Guards,' my father said. My grand-mothers couldn't touch their fried eggs, so that was more food wasted. It was the worst evening of my grandmothers' lives.

'There was an understanding between us.' She would stand there for ever, I thought, looking at me like that, as still as stone while my father tediously gabbled.

'Keep off the drink, boy,' he commanded, having issued other orders, as well as warnings and advice. 'You're too young for that game.'

'I'm going to work in the picture house.'

The vituperation I had anticipated burst simultaneously out of them, scornful and immediate. Their faces reddened. My father pushed himself on to his feet.

'I don't like it in the timberyard,' I said.

'What don't you like, boy?'

'I don't like any of it.'

'You're a young pup. Haven't you caused enough damage for one day? Go up and knock on your grandmothers' doors and tell them you're safe and sound. The other stuff you're talking about is rubbish.'

I went away, glad to be allowed to do so. Obediently I knocked on my grandmothers' doors, but there was no response from either of them, as I had known there wouldn't be. In my own room I sat on the edge of my bed and within a few moments I felt tears on my cheeks. In the dining-room they would be deploring my defiance, saying they could not control me, that I had always been like that, a bad example to my brothers. There had been pain in my father's eyes, and in the bluster of his voice when he'd called me a young pup, but I didn't care; I didn't care in the least how much I hurt them. It was like a nightmare, that she was going to die.

5

Slowly, carefully, she passed upstairs to the balcony, holding on to her husband's arm. And when *Rebecca* came to an end they left the cinema in the same unhurried manner. There was, I realise now, nothing she might have said to me, and I could tell from her expression that she found it difficult to smile. 'Please wait,' Herr Messinger had requested when he'd set out my duties for that evening. He returned some time later, and together we locked up his property. 'One day I shall place you in charge of the Alexandra,' he said. He paused, and added: 'That is her wish, and my own too.'

I would have carried the wireless battery out to Cloverhill as I had before, but that was not suggested. At a quarter past ten every night Herr Messinger arrived in his gas-powered motor-car and stood on the marble steps, ready to say goodnight to his customers when the film ended. I believe, although I cannot be certain, that she asked him to. When everyone had gone I would give him the cash-box and he would drive away again.

Three times a week I fetched the films in their metal cases from the railway station and returned those that had been shown, the smaller cases containing the newsreels and the shorts, another episode of *Flaming Frontiers* or *The Torture Chamber of Doctor R.* Every evening, and during the Sunday matinee, I sat in the projection room with the old man who had been the projectionist in some other town, whom Herr Messinger had brought back into employment. When the old man's stomach gave him trouble and he wasn't able to come in I took his place, as soon as there was no further custom at the box-office.

'For the sake of your mother,' my father pleaded, 'wouldn't you have a bit of sense for yourself?'

He meant wouldn't I stop doing what I was content to do and return to the drabness of the timberyard. I was becoming a queer type of a fellow, he told me, which wasn't a good thing for a mother to have to see. 'Come into Viney's one day and we'll have a bottle of stout over it,' he invited, forgetting his advice to me with regard to drinking in public houses.

Politely, I thanked him and said I'd look into Viney's when I had a moment to spare, not intending to and in fact never doing so. On the balcony stairs there were framed photographs of William Powell and Myrna Loy, of Loretta Young and Carole Lombard and Norma Shearer, of Franchot Tone and Lew Ayres. I could see some of them from the box-office and used to watch people stopping to examine them, couples arm in arm, the girls' voices full of wonder. In the mornings I opened the exit doors at the back, on either side of the screen, in order to let the fresh air in for an hour or two. When the woman who swept the place out didn't arrive I did it myself; I mopped the foyer and the steps, and went over the carpets with the suction cleaner. Often in the mornings I would press the switch that caused the yellow and green curtains that obscured the screen to open, the butterflies of the pattern disappearing as the curtains moved. When the daylight came in through the exit doors the amber shading of the walls seemed different.

People loved the Alexandra. They loved the things I loved myself – the scarlet seats, the lights that made the curtains change colour, the usherettes in uniform. People stood smoking in the foyer when they'd bought their tickets, not in a hurry because smoking and talking gave them pleasure also. They loved the luxury of the Alexandra, they loved the place it was. Urney bars tasted better in its rosy gloom; embraces were romantic there. Fred Astaire and Ginger Rogers shared their sophisticated dreams, Deanna Durbin sang. Heroes fell from horses, the sagas of great families yielded the riches of their secrets. Night after night in the Alexandra I stood at the back, aware of the pleasure I dealt in, feeling it all around me. Shoulders slumped, heads touched, eyes were lost in concentration. My brothers did not snigger in the Alexandra: my father, had he ever gone there, would have at last been silenced. Often I imagined the tetchiness of the Reverend Wauchope softening beneath a weight of wonder, and the sour disposition of his wife lifted from her as she watched *All This and Heaven Too*. Often I imagined the complicated shame fading from the features of Mr Conron. 'I have told her you are happy,' Herr Messinger said.

Annie began to come to the cinema with young Phelan from Phelan's grocery, in whose presence she was less sullen. She showed him off, one eye on me in the box-office, pausing on the balcony stairs and calling out loudly to people she knew. She had begun to wear different shades of lipstick, and had her hair done in a different way. For all my good fortune in being sent away to school, and my escape from the timberyard, she would outdo me in the end. She was outdoing me already, her manner implied, standing close to young Phelan.

A month before the war ended the death took place at Clover-hill House. Herr Messinger did not mention it but I knew it had occurred because he arrived at the cinema in mourning, and two days later there was the funeral, her body taken to our Protestant graveyard. He made arrangements about the sale of his land and the running of the cinema, placing certain matters in the hands of McDonagh and Effingham, the solicitors, others in the care of the Munster and Leinster Bank. It was not clear then that one day I would become the cinema's proprietor, that arrangements had been made in this respect also. 'I'd say you landed on your feet,' my father grudgingly remarked when the big attendances the cinema had begun to attract showed no sign of abating, but my mother never forgave me for rejecting my heritage in favour of selling tickets, and for ignoring her wishes. When my mother lay dying in 1961 she referred again to Frau Messinger as a wanton and a strumpet, whose grave she knew I tended, growing anemones on the humped earth.

My mother was right when she sensed the need to be jealous.

Frau Messinger had claimed me from the moment she stepped from her husband's car that day in Laffan Street: and she had held me to her with the story of her life. Details that were lost in the enchantment of her voice return with time. How when she was five she picked a flower from a garden where she was a visitor, and afterwards felt a thief. How she overheard servants being cruel about her mother. How she had bathed in a shrubbery lake, before anyone else was up, the water so petrifyingly cold she'd thought she could not bear it. How the old man said to her the first time she met him, in a German bookshop furnished like a drawing-room: 'Have you read *Wanderers Nachtlied*?' She hadn't even heard of it, and blushed with shame.

I retrieved her present from the crevice in the step at Cloverhill. All the windows already had boards on them, efficiently nailed into place, as though Herr Messinger wished to keep the contents of the house exactly as they were, unaffected even by sunlight. The land was sold and farmed by someone else; Daphie went to work for other people. I was given the task – for which I was remunerated once a month through the solicitors – of seeing that the window boards remained in place and were renewed when necessary, and that the doors were kept secure. It was everyone's belief – the solicitors', the bank's, his employees' at the cinema – that Herr Messinger intended to return, that once again he would root out the brambles from the garden and let light into the drawing-room. I knew he never would. He could not be alone in Cloverhill. In Germany he would be hopelessly searching for his sons.

6

My brothers run the timberyard, my sister married Phelan, my father went the way of my mother and my grandmothers. I do not forget those family mealtimes, the half bottle of whiskey kept in the sideboard in case anyone had toothache, holly poked behind the pictures at Christmas. I do not forget my companions of the rectory bedroom, nor poor obese Lottie Belle, who did not then seem worthy of compassion. I do not forget them, but even so I do not dwell much on those particular memories. Is such love reserved for the dying? I ask myself instead, and do not know the answer.

Years ago the butterfly curtains had to be taken down because they were rotting. When you listen with your ear to the boarded windows of Cloverhill you can hear the rats inside. One day next week men will place corrugated iron over the entrance to the cinema, and over the exit doors at the back. I shall not sell the place, even though I have been tempted with a fair price from a business partnership that would turn it into a furniture store; in the town I am considered foolhardy because I have rejected this offer. I am considered odd, being so often seen on the Ballinadee road on my way to tap the window boards, making certain they are sound. In the town it is said that the cinema has destroyed me, that I'd have been better off if I'd never inherited it in that peculiar way. My sister and brothers have said it to my face, others have whispered. I am pitied because I am solitary and withdrawn, because I have not taken my place and am left in the end with nothing. I have no answer.

It is sad that through a quirk of fashion no one came much to the Alexandra these last few years. It is sad that rats are in charge at Cloverhill. But a husband's love and a woman's gratitude for sanctuary have not surrendered their potency. I am a fifty-eight-year-old cinema proprietor without a cinema, yet when I sit among the empty seats memory is enough. She smiles from the green-striped cushions, he spreads his drawings on the floor. My rain-soaked clothes drip on to the fender by the fire, there is happiness in spite of death and war. Fate has made me the ghost of an interlude: once in a while I say that in the town, trying to explain.

The Ballroom of Romance

On Sundays, or on Mondays if he couldn't make it and often he couldn't, Sunday being his busy day, Canon O'Connell arrived at the farm in order to hold a private service with Bridie's father, who couldn't get about any more, having had a leg amputated after gangrene had set in. They'd had a pony and cart then and Bridie's mother had been alive: it hadn't been difficult for the two of them to help her father on to the cart in order to make the journey to Mass. But two years later the pony had gone lame and eventually had to be destroyed; not long after that her mother had died. 'Don't worry about it at all,' Canon O'Connell had said, referring to the difficulty of transporting her father to Mass. 'I'll slip up by the week, Bridie.'

The milk lorry called daily for the single churn of milk, Mr Driscoll delivered groceries and meal in his van, and took away the eggs that Bridie had collected during the week. Since Canon O'Connell had made his offer, in 1953, Bridie's father hadn't left the farm.

As well as Mass on Sundays and her weekly visits to a wayside dance-hall Bridie went shopping once every month, cycling to the town early on a Friday afternoon. She bought things for herself, material for a dress, knitting wool, stockings, a newspaper, and paper-backed Wild West novels for her father. She talked in the shops to some of the girls she'd been at school with, girls who had married shop-assistants or shopkeepers, or had become assistants themselves. Most of them had families of their own by now. 'You're lucky to be peaceful in the hills,' they said to Bridie, 'instead of stuck in a hole like this.' They had a tired look, most of them, from pregnancies and their efforts to organise and control their large families.

As she cycled back to the hills on a Friday Bridie often felt that they truly envied her her life, and she found it surprising that they should do so. If it hadn't been for her father she'd have wanted to work in the town also, in the tinned-meat factory maybe, or in a shop. The town had a cinema called the Electric, and a fish-and-chip shop where people met at night, eating chips out of newspaper on the pavement outside. In the evenings, sitting in the farmhouse with her father, she often thought about the town, imagining the shop-windows lit up to display their goods and the sweet-shops still open so that people could purchase chocolates or fruit to take with them to the Electric cinema. But the town was eleven miles away, which was too far to cycle, there and back, for an evening's entertainment.

'It's a terrible thing for you, girl,' her father used to say, genuinely troubled, 'tied up to a one-legged man.' He would sigh heavily, hobbling back from the fields, where he managed as best he could. 'If your mother hadn't died,' he'd say, not finishing the sentence.

If her mother hadn't died her mother could have looked after him and the scant acres he owned, her mother could somehow have lifted the milk-churn on to the collection platform and attended to the few hens and the cows. 'I'd be dead without the girl to assist me,' she'd heard her father saying to Canon O'Connell, and Canon O'Connell replied that he was certainly lucky to have her.

'Amn't I as happy here as anywhere?' she'd say herself, but her father knew she was pretending and was saddened because the weight of circumstances had so harshly interfered with her life.

Although her father still called her a girl, Bridie was thirty-six. She was tall and strong: the skin of her fingers and her palms was stained, and harsh to touch. The labour they'd experienced had found its way into them, as though juices had come out of vegetation and pigment out of soil: since childhood she'd torn away the rough scotch grass that grew each spring among her father's mangolds and sugar-beet; since childhood she'd harvested

64

potatoes in August, her hands daily rooting in the ground she loosened and turned. Wind had toughened the flesh of her face, sun had browned it; her neck and nose were lean, her lips touched with early wrinkles.

But on Saturday nights Bridie forgot the scotch grass and the soil. In different dresses she cycled to the dance-hall, encouraged to make the journey by her father. 'Doesn't it do you good, girl?' he'd say, as though he imagined she begrudged herself the pleasure. 'Why wouldn't you enjoy yourself?' She'd cook him his tea and then he'd settle down with the wireless, or maybe a Wild West novel. In time, while still she danced, he'd stoke the fire up and hobble his way upstairs to bed.

The dance-hall, owned by Mr Justin Dwyer, was miles from anywhere, a long building by the roadside with treeless boglands all around and a gravel expanse in front of it. On pink pebbled cement its title was painted in an azure blue that matched the depth of the background shade yet stood out well, unfussily proclaiming *The Ballroom of Romance*. Above these letters four coloured bulbs – in red, green, orange and mauve – were lit at appropriate times, an indication that the evening rendezvous was open for business. Only the façade of the building was pink, the other walls being a more ordinary grey. And inside, except for pink swing-doors, everything was blue.

On Saturday nights Mr Justin Dwyer, a small, thin man, unlocked the metal grid that protected his property and drew it back, creating an open mouth from which music would later pour. He helped his wife to carry crates of lemonade and packets of biscuits from their car, and then took up a position in the tiny vestibule between the drawn-back grid and the pink swing-doors. He sat at a card-table, with money and tickets spread out before him. He'd made a fortune, people said: he owned other ballrooms also.

People came on bicycles or in old motor-cars, country people like Bridie from remote hill farms and villages. People who did not often see other people met there, girls and boys, men and women. They paid Mr Dwyer and passed into his dance-hall, where shadows were cast on pale-blue walls and light from a crystal bowl was dim. The band, known as the Romantic Jazz Band, was composed of clarinet, drums and piano. The drummer sometimes sang.

Bridie had been going to the dance-hall since first she left the Presentation Nuns, before her mother's death. She didn't mind the journey, which was seven miles there and seven back: she'd travelled as far every day to the Presentation Nuns on the same bicycle, which had once been the property of her mother, an old Rudge purchased originally in 1936. On Sundays she cycled six miles to Mass, but she never minded either: she'd grown quite used to all that.

'How're you, Bridie?' enquired Mr Justin Dwyer when she arrived in a new scarlet dress one autumn evening. She said she was all right and in reply to Mr Dwyer's second query she said that her father was all right also. 'I'll go up one of these days,' promised Mr Dwyer, which was a promise he'd been making for twenty years.

She paid the entrance fee and passed through the pink swing-doors. The Romantic Jazz Band was playing a familiar melody of the past, 'The Destiny Waltz'. In spite of the band's title, jazz was not ever played in the ballroom: Mr Dwyer did not personally care for that kind of music, nor had he cared for various dance movements that had come and gone over the years. Jiving, rock and roll, twisting and other such variations had all been resisted by Mr Dwyer, who believed that a ballroom should be, as much as possible, a dignified place. The Romantic Jazz Band consisted of Mr Maloney, Mr Swanton, and Dano Ryan on drums. They were three middle-aged men who drove out from the town in Mr Maloney's car, amateur performers who were employed otherwise by the tinned-meat factory, the Electricity Supply Board and the County Council.

'How're you, Bridie?' enquired Dano Ryan as she passed him on her way to the cloakroom. He was idle for a moment with his drums, 'The Destiny Waltz' not calling for much attention from him.

'I'm all right, Dano,' she said. 'Are you fit yourself? Are the eyes better?' The week before he'd told her that he'd developed a watering of the eyes that must have been some kind of cold or other. He'd woken up with it in the morning and it had persisted until the afternoon: it was a new experience, he'd told her, adding that he'd never had a day's illness or discomfort in his life.

'I think I need glasses,' he said now, and as she passed into the cloakroom she imagined him in glasses, repairing the roads, as he was employed to do by the County Council. You hardly ever saw a road-mender with glasses, she reflected, and she wondered if all the dust that was inherent in his work had perhaps affected his eyes.

'How're you, Bridie?' a girl called Eenie Mackie said in the cloakroom, a girl who'd left the Presentation Nuns only a year ago.

'That's a lovely dress, Eenie,' Bridie said. 'Is it nylon, that?'

'Tricel actually. Drip-dry.'

Bridie took off her coat and hung it on a hook. There was a small wash-basin in the cloakroom above which hung a discoloured oval mirror. Used tissues and pieces of cotton-wool, cigarette-butts and matches covered the concrete floor. Lengths of green-painted timber partitioned off a lavatory in a corner.

'Jeez, you're looking great, Bridie,' Madge Dowding remarked, waiting for her turn at the mirror. She moved towards it as she spoke, taking off a pair of spectacles before endeavouring to apply make-up to the lashes of her eye. She stared myopically into the oval mirror, humming while the other girls became restive.

'Will you hurry up, for God's sake!' shouted Eenie Mackie. 'We're standing here all night, Madge.'

Madge Dowding was the only one who was older than Bridie. She was thirty-nine, although often she said she was younger. The girls sniggered about that, saying that Madge Dowding should accept her condition – her age and her squint and her poor complexion – and not make herself ridiculous going out after men. What man would be bothered with the like of her anyway? Madge Dowding would do better to give herself over to do Saturday-night work for the Legion of Mary: wasn't Canon O'Connell always looking for aid?

'Is that fellow there?' she asked now, moving away from the mirror. 'The guy with the long arms. Did anyone see him outside?'

'He's dancing with Cat Bolger,' one of the girls replied. 'She has herself glued to him.'

'Lover boy,' remarked Patty Byrne, and everyone laughed because the person referred to was hardly a boy any more, being over fifty it was said, a bachelor who came only occasionally to the dance-hall.

Madge Dowding left the cloakroom rapidly, not bothering to pretend she wasn't anxious about the conjunction of Cat Bolger and the man with the long arms. Two sharp spots of red had come into her cheeks, and when she stumbled in her haste the girls in the cloakroom laughed. A younger girl would have pretended to be casual.

Bridie chatted, waiting for the mirror. Some girls, not wishing to be delayed, used the mirrors of their compacts. Then in twos and threes, occasionally singly, they left the cloakroom and took their places on upright wooden chairs at one end of the dance-hall, waiting to be asked to dance. Mr Maloney, Mr Swanton and Dano Ryan played 'Harvest Moon' and 'I Wonder Who's Kissing Her Now' and 'I'll Be Around'.

Bridie danced. Her father would be falling asleep by the fire; the wireless, tuned in to Radio Eireann, would be murmuring in the background. Already he'd have listened to *Faith and Order* and *Spot the Talent*. His Wild West novel, *Three Rode Fast* by Jake Matall, would have dropped from his single knee on to the flagged floor. He would wake with a jerk as he did every night and, forgetting what night it was, might be surprised not to see her, for usually she was sitting there at the table, mending clothes or washing eggs. 'Is it time for the news?' he'd automatically say.

Dust and cigarette smoke formed a haze beneath the crystal bowl, feet thudded, girls shrieked and laughed, some of them dancing together for want of a male partner. The music was loud, the musicians had taken off their jackets. Vigorously they played a number of tunes from *State Fair* and then, more romantically, 'Just One of Those Things'. The tempo increased for a Paul Jones, after which Bridie found herself with a youth who told her he was saving up to emigrate, the nation in his opinion being finished. 'I'm up in the hills with the uncle,' he said, 'labouring fourteen hours a day. Is it any life for a young fellow?' She knew his uncle, a hill farmer whose stony acres were separated from her father's by one other farm only. 'He has me gutted with work,' the youth told her. 'Is there sense in it at all, Bridie?'

At ten o'clock there was a stir, occasioned by the arrival of three middle-aged bachelors who'd cycled over from Carey's public house. They shouted and whistled, greeting other people across the dancing area. They smelt of stout and sweat and whiskey.

Every Saturday at just this time they arrived, and, having sold them their tickets, Mr Dwyer folded up his card-table and locked the tin box that held the evening's takings: his ballroom was complete.

'How're you, Bridie?' one of the bachelors, known as Bowser Egan, enquired. Another one, Tim Daly, asked Patty Byrne how she was. 'Will we take the floor?' Eyes Horgan suggested to Madge Dowding, already pressing the front of his navy-blue suit against the net of her dress. Bridie danced with Bowser Egan, who said she was looking great.

The bachelors would never marry, the girls of the dance-hall considered: they were wedded already, to stout and whiskey and laziness, to three old mothers somewhere up in the hills. The man with the long arms didn't drink but he was the same in all other ways: he had the same look of a bachelor, a quality in his face.

'Great,' Bowser Egan said, feather-stepping in an inaccurate and inebriated manner. 'You're a great little dancer, Bridie.'

'Will you lay off that!' cried Madge Dowding, her voice shrill above the sound of the music. Eyes Horgan had slipped two fingers into the back of her dress and was now pretending they'd got there by accident. He smiled blearily, his huge red face streaming with perspiration, the eyes which gave him his nickname protuberant and bloodshot.

'Watch your step with that one,' Bowser Egan called out, laughing so that spittle sprayed on to Bridie's face. Eenie Mackie, who was also dancing near the incident, laughed also and winked at Bridie. Dano Ryan left his drums and sang. 'Oh, how I miss your gentle kiss,' he crooned, 'and long to hold you tight.'

Nobody knew the name of the man with the long arms. The only words he'd ever been known to speak in the Ballroom of Romance were the words that formed his invitation to dance. He was a shy man who stood alone when he wasn't performing on the dance-floor. He rode away on his bicycle afterwards, not saying goodnight to anyone.

'Cat has your man leppin' tonight,' Tim Daly remarked to Patty Byrne, for the liveliness that Cat Bolger had introduced into foxtrot and waltz was noticeable.

'I think of you only,' sang Dano Ryan. 'Only wishing, wishing you were by my side.'

Dano Ryan would have done, Bridie often thought, because he was a different kind of bachelor: he had a lonely look about him, as if he'd become tired of being on his own. Every week she thought he would have done, and during the week her mind regularly returned to that thought. Dano Ryan would have done because she felt he wouldn't mind coming to live in the farmhouse while her one-legged father was still about the place. Three could live as cheaply as two where Dano Ryan was concerned because giving up the wages he earned as a road-worker would be balanced by the saving made on what he paid for lodgings. Once, at the end of an evening, she'd pretended that there was a puncture in the back wheel of her bicycle and he'd concerned himself with it while Mr Maloney and Mr Swanton waited for him in Mr Maloney's car. He'd blown the tyre up with the car pump and had said he thought it would hold.

It was well known in the dance-hall that she fancied her chances with Dano Ryan. But it was well known also that Dano Ryan had got into a set way of life and had remained in it for quite some years. He lodged with a widow called Mrs Griffin and Mrs Griffin's mentally affected son, in a cottage on the outskirts of the town. He was said to be good to the affected child, buying him sweets and taking him out for rides on the crossbar of his bicycle. He gave an hour or two of his time every week to the Church of Our Lady Queen of Heaven, and he was loyal to Mr Dwyer. He performed in the two other rural dance-halls that Mr Dwyer owned, rejecting advances from the town's more sophisticated dance-hall, even though it was more conveniently situated for him and the fee was more substantial than that paid by Mr Dwyer. But Mr Dwyer had discovered Dano Ryan and Dano had not forgotten it, just as Mr Maloney and Mr Swanton had not forgotten their discovery by Mr Dwyer either.

'Would we take a lemonade?' Bowser Egan suggested. 'And a packet of biscuits, Bridie?'

No alcoholic liquor was ever served in the Ballroom of Romance, the premises not being licensed for this added stimulant. Mr Dwyer in fact had never sought a licence for any of his premises, knowing that romance and alcohol were difficult commodities to mix, especially in a dignified ballroom. Behind where the girls sat on the wooden chairs Mr Dwyer's wife, a small stout woman, served the bottles of lemonade, with straws, and the biscuits, and crisps. She talked busily while doing so, mainly about the turkeys she kept. She'd once told Bridie that she thought of them as children.

'Thanks,' Bridie said, and Bowser Egan led her to the trestle table. Soon it would be the intermission: soon the three members of the band would cross the floor also for refreshment. She thought up questions to ask Dano Ryan.

When first she'd danced in the Ballroom of Romance, when

she was just sixteen, Dano Ryan had been there also, four years older than she was, playing the drums for Mr Maloney as he played them now. She'd hardly noticed him then because of his not being one of the dancers: he was part of the ballroom's scenery, like the trestle table and the lemonade bottles, and Mrs Dwyer and Mr Dwyer. The youths who'd danced with her then in their Saturday-night blue suits had later disappeared into the town, or to Dublin or Britain, leaving behind them those who became the middle-aged bachelors of the hills. There'd been a boy called Patrick Grady whom she had loved in those days. Week after week she'd ridden away from the Ballroom of Romance with the image of his face in her mind, a thin face, pale beneath black hair. It had been different, dancing with Patrick Grady, and she'd felt that he found it different dancing with her, although he'd never said so. At night she'd dreamed of him and in the daytime too, while she helped her mother in the kitchen or her father with the cows. Week by week she'd returned to the ballroom, delighting in its pink façade and dancing in the arms of Patrick Grady. Often they'd stood together drinking lemonade, not saying anything, not knowing what to say. She knew he loved her, and she believed then that he would lead her one day from the dim, romantic ballroom, from its blueness and its pinkness and its crystal bowl of light and its music. She believed he would lead her into sunshine, to the town and the Church of Our Lady Queen of Heaven, to marriage and smiling faces. But someone else had got Patrick Grady, a girl from the town who'd never danced in the wayside ballroom. She'd scooped up Patrick Grady when he didn't have a chance.

Bridie had wept, hearing that. By night she'd lain in her bed in the farmhouse, quietly crying, the tears rolling into her hair and making the pillow damp. When she woke in the early morning the thought was still naggingly with her and it remained with her by day, replacing her daytime dreams of happiness. Someone told her later on that he'd crossed to Britain, to Wolverhampton, with the girl he'd married, and she imagined him there, in a place she wasn't able properly to visualise, labouring in a factory, his children being born and acquiring the accent of the area. The Ballroom of Romance wasn't the same without him, and when no one else stood out for her particularly over the years and when no one offered her marriage, she found herself wondering about Dano Ryan. If you couldn't have love, the next best thing was surely a decent man.

Bowser Egan hardly fell into that category, nor did Tim Daly. And it was plain to everyone that Cat Bolger and Madge Dowding were wasting their time over the man with the long arms. Madge Dowding was already a figure of fun in the ballroom, the way she ran after the bachelors; Cat Bolger would end up the same if she wasn't careful. One way or another it wasn't difficult to be a figure of fun in the ballroom, and you didn't have to be as old as Madge Dowding: a girl who'd just left the Presentation Nuns had once asked Eyes Horgan what he had in his trouser pocket and he told her it was a penknife. She'd repeated this afterwards in the cloakroom, how she'd requested Eyes Horgan not to dance so close to her because his penknife was sticking into her. 'Jeez, aren't you the right baby!' Patty Byrne had shouted delightedly; everyone had laughed, knowing that Eyes Horgan only came to the ballroom for stuff like that. He was no use to any girl.

'Two lemonades, Mrs Dwyer,' Bowser Egan said, 'and two packets of Kerry Creams. Is Kerry Creams all right, Bridie?'

She nodded, smiling. Kerry Creams would be fine, she said.

'Well, Bridie, isn't that the great outfit you have!' Mrs Dwyer remarked. 'Doesn't the red suit her, Bowser?'

By the swing-doors stood Mr Dwyer, smoking a cigarette that he held cupped in his left hand. His small eyes noted all developments. He had been aware of Madge Dowding's anxiety when Eyes Horgan had inserted two fingers into the back opening of her dress. He had looked away, not caring for the incident, but had it developed further he would have spoken to Eyes Horgan, as he had on other occasions. Some of the younger lads didn't know any better and would dance very close to their partners, who generally were too embarrassed to do anything about it, being young themselves. But that, in Mr Dwyer's opinion, was a different kettle of fish altogether because they were decent young lads who'd in no time at all be doing a steady line with a girl and would end up as he had himself with Mrs Dwyer, in the same house with her, sleeping in a bed with her, firmly married. It was the middle-aged bachelors who required the watching: they came down from the hills like mountain goats, released from their mammies and from the smell of animals and soil. Mr Dwyer continued to watch Eyes Horgan, wondering how drunk he was.

Dano Ryan's song came to an end, Mr Swanton laid down his clarinet, Mr Maloney rose from the piano. Dano Ryan wiped sweat from his face and the three men slowly moved towards Mrs Dwyer's trestle table.

'Jeez, you have powerful legs,' Eyes Horgan whispered to Madge Dowding, but Madge Dowding's attention was on the man with the long arms, who had left Cat Bolger's side and was proceeding in the direction of the men's lavatory. He never took refreshments. She moved, herself, towards the men's lavatory, to take up a position outside it, but Eyes Horgan followed her. 'Would you take a lemonade, Madge?' he asked. He had a small bottle of whiskey on him: if they went into a corner they could add a drop of it to the lemonade. She didn't drink spirits, she reminded him, and he went away.

'Excuse me a minute,' Bowser Egan said, putting down his bottle of lemonade. He crossed the floor to the lavatory. He too, Bridie knew, would have a small bottle of whiskey on him. She watched while Dano Ryan, listening to a story Mr Maloney was telling, paused in the centre of the ballroom, his head bent to hear what was being said. He was a big man, heavily made, with black hair that was slightly touched with grey, and big hands. He laughed when Mr Maloney came to the end of his story and then bent his head again, in order to listen to a story told by Mr Swanton.

'Are you on your own, Bridie?' Cat Bolger asked, and Bridie

said she was waiting for Bowser Egan. 'I think I'll have a lemonade,' Cat Bolger said.

Younger boys and girls stood with their arms still around one another, queuing up for refreshments. Boys who hadn't danced at all, being nervous because they didn't know any steps, stood in groups, smoking and making jokes. Girls who hadn't been danced with yet talked to one another, their eyes wandering. Some of them sucked at straws in lemonade bottles.

Bridie, still watching Dano Ryan, imagined him wearing the glasses he'd referred to, sitting in the farmhouse kitchen, reading one of her father's Wild West novels. She imagined the three of them eating a meal she'd prepared, fried eggs and rashers and fried potato-cakes, and tea and bread and butter and jam, brown bread and soda and shop bread. She imagined Dano Ryan leaving the kitchen in the morning to go out to the fields in order to weed the mangolds, and her father hobbling off behind him, and the two men working together. She saw hay being cut, Dano Ryan with the scythe that she'd learnt to use herself, her father using a rake as best he could. She saw herself, because of the extra help, being able to attend to things in the farmhouse, things she'd never had time for because of the cows and the hens and the fields. There were bedroom curtains that needed repairing where the net had ripped, and wallpaper that had become loose and needed to be stuck up with flour paste. The scullery required white-washing.

The night he'd blown up the tyre of her bicycle she'd thought he was going to kiss her. He'd crouched on the ground in the darkness with his ear to the tyre, listening for escaping air. When he could hear none he'd straightened up and said he thought she'd be all right on the bicycle. His face had been quite close to hers and she'd smiled at him. At that moment, unfortunately, Mr Maloney had blown an impatient blast on the horn of his motor-car.

Often she'd been kissed by Bowser Egan, on the nights when he insisted on riding part of the way home with her. They had to dismount in order to push their bicycles up a hill and the first time he'd accompanied her he'd contrived to fall against her, steadying himself by putting a hand on her shoulder. The next thing she was aware of was the moist quality of his lips and the sound of his bicycle as it clattered noisily on the road. He'd suggested then, regaining his breath, that they should go into a field.

That was nine years ago. In the intervening passage of time she'd been kissed as well, in similar circumstances, by Eyes Horgan and Tim Daly. She'd gone into fields with them and permitted them to put their arms about her while heavily they breathed. At one time or another she had imagined marriage with one or other of them, seeing them in the farmhouse with her father, even though the fantasies were unlikely.

Bridie stood with Cat Bolger, knowing that it would be some time before Bowser Egan came out of the lavatory. Mr Maloney, Mr Swanton and Dano Ryan approached, Mr Maloney insisting that he would fetch three bottles of lemonade from the trestle table.

'You sang the last one beautifully,' Bridie said to Dano Ryan. 'Isn't it a beautiful song?'

Mr Swanton said it was the finest song ever written, and Cat Bolger said she preferred 'Danny Boy', which in her opinion was the finest song ever written.

'Take a suck of that,' said Mr Maloney, handing Dano Ryan and Mr Swanton bottles of lemonade. 'How's Bridie tonight? Is your father well, Bridie?'

Her father was all right, she said.

'I hear they're starting a cement factory,' said Mr Maloney. 'Did anyone hear talk of that? They're after striking some commodity in the earth that makes good cement. Ten feet down, over at Kilmalough.'

'It'll bring employment,' said Mr Swanton. 'It's employment that's necessary in this area.'

'Canon O'Connell was on about it,' Mr Maloney said. 'There's Yankee money involved.'

'Will the Yanks come over?' enquired Cat Bolger. 'Will they run it themselves, Mr Maloney?'

Mr Maloney, intent on his lemonade, didn't hear the questions and Cat Bolger didn't repeat them.

'There's stuff called Optrex,' Bridie said quietly to Dano Ryan, 'that my father took the time he had a cold in his eyes. Maybe Optrex would settle the watering, Dano.'

'Ah sure, it doesn't worry me that much –'

'It's terrible, anything wrong with the eyes. You wouldn't want to take a chance. You'd get Optrex in a chemist, Dano, and a little bowl with it so that you can bathe the eyes.'

Her father's eyes had become red-rimmed and unsightly to look at. She'd gone into Riordan's Medical Hall in the town and had explained what the trouble was, and Mr Riordan had recommended Optrex. She told this to Dano Ryan, adding that her father had had no trouble with his eyes since. Dano Ryan nodded.

'Did you hear that, Mrs Dwyer?' Mr Maloney called out. 'A cement factory for Kilmalough.'

Mrs Dwyer wagged her head, placing empty bottles in a crate. She'd heard references to the cement factory, she said: it was the best news for a long time.

'Kilmalough won't know itself,' her husband commented, joining her in her task with the empty lemonade bottles.

''Twill bring prosperity certainly,' said Mr Swanton. 'I was saying just there, Justin, that employment's what's necessary.'

'Sure, won't the Yanks –' began Cat Bolger, but Mr Maloney interrupted her.

'The Yanks'll be in at the top, Cat, or maybe not here at all – maybe only inserting money into it. It'll be local labour entirely.'

'You'll not marry a Yank, Cat,' said Mr Swanton, loudly laughing. 'You can't catch those fellows.'

'Haven't you plenty of homemade bachelors?' suggested Mr Maloney. He laughed also, throwing away the straw he was sucking through and tipping the bottle into his mouth. Cat Bolger told him to get on with himself. She moved towards the men's lavatory and took up a position outside it, not speaking to Madge Dowding, who was still standing there.

'Keep a watch on Eyes Horgan,' Mrs Dwyer warned her husband, which was advice she gave him at this time every Saturday night, knowing that Eyes Horgan was drinking in the lavatory. When he was drunk Eyes Horgan was the most difficult of the bachelors.

'I have a drop of it left, Dano,' Bridie said quietly. 'I could bring it over on Saturday. The eye stuff.'

'Ah, don't worry yourself, Bridie –'

'No trouble at all. Honestly now –'

'Mrs Griffin has me fixed up for a test with Dr Cready. The old eyes are no worry, only when I'm reading the paper or at the pictures. Mrs Griffin says I'm only straining them due to lack of glasses.'

He looked away while he said that, and she knew at once that Mrs Griffin was arranging to marry him. She felt it instinctively: Mrs Griffin was going to marry him because she was afraid that if he moved away from her cottage, to get married to someone else, she'd find it hard to replace him with another lodger who'd be good to her affected son. He'd become a father to Mrs Griffin's affected son, to whom already he was kind. It was a natural outcome, for Mrs Griffin had all the chances, seeing him every night and morning and not having to make do with weekly encounters in a ballroom.

She thought of Patrick Grady, seeing in her mind his pale, thin face. She might be the mother of four of his children now, or seven or eight maybe. She might be living in Wolverhampton, going out to the pictures in the evenings, instead of looking after a one-legged man. If the weight of circumstances hadn't intervened she wouldn't be standing in a wayside ballroom, mourning the marriage of a road-mender she didn't love. For a moment she thought she might cry, standing there thinking of Patrick Grady in Wolverhampton. In her life, on the farm and in the house, there was no place for tears. Tears were a luxury, like flowers would be in the fields where the mangolds grew, or fresh white-wash in the scullery. It wouldn't have been fair ever to have wept in the kitchen while her father sat listening to *Spot the Talent*: her father had more right to weep, having lost a leg. He suffered in a greater way, yet he remained kind and concerned for her.

In the Ballroom of Romance she felt behind her eyes the tears that it would have been improper to release in the presence of her father. She wanted to let them go, to feel them streaming on her cheeks, to receive the sympathy of Dano Ryan and of everyone else. She wanted them all to listen to her while she told them about Patrick Grady who was now in Wolverhampton and about the death of her mother and her own life since. She wanted Dano Ryan to put his arm around her so that she could lean her head against it. She wanted him to look at her in his decent way and to stroke with his road-mender's fingers the backs of her hands. She might wake in a bed with him and imagine for a moment that he was Patrick Grady. She might bathe his eyes and pretend.

'Back to business,' said Mr Maloney, leading his band across the floor to their instruments.

'Tell your father I was asking for him,' Dano Ryan said. She smiled and she promised, as though nothing had happened, that she would tell her father that.

She danced with Tim Daly and then again with the youth who'd said he intended to emigrate. She saw Madge Dowding moving swiftly towards the man with the long arms as he came out of the lavatory, moving faster than Cat Bolger. Eyes Horgan approached Cat Bolger. Dancing with her, he spoke earnestly, attempting to persuade her to permit him to ride part of the way home with her. He was unaware of the jealousy that was coming from her as she watched Madge Dowding holding close to her the man with the long arms while they performed a quickstep. Cat Bolger was in her thirties also.

'Get away out of that,' said Bowser Egan, cutting in on the youth who was dancing with Bridie. 'Go home to your mammy, boy.' He took her into his arms, saying again that she was looking great tonight. 'Did you hear about the cement factory?' he said. 'Isn't it great for Kilmalough?'

She agreed. She said what Mr Swanton and Mr Maloney had said: that the cement factory would bring employment to the neighbourhood.

'Will I ride home with you a bit, Bridie?' Bowser Egan suggested, and she pretended not to hear him. 'Aren't you my girl, Bridie, and always have been?' he said, a statement that made no sense at all.

His voice went on whispering at her, saying he would marry her tomorrow only his mother wouldn't permit another woman in the house. She knew what it was like herself, he reminded her, having a parent to look after: you couldn't leave them to rot, you had to honour your father and your mother.

She danced to 'The Bells Are Ringing', moving her legs in time with Bowser Egan's while over his shoulder she watched Dano Ryan softly striking one of his smaller drums. Mrs Griffin had got him even though she was nearly fifty, with no looks at all, a lumpish woman with lumpish legs and arms. Mrs Griffin had got him just as the girl had got Patrick Grady.

The music ceased, Bowser Egan held her hard against him, trying to touch her face with his. Around them, people whistled and clapped: the evening had come to an end. She walked away from Bowser Egan, knowing that not ever again would she dance in the Ballroom of Romance. She'd been a figure of fun, trying to promote a relationship with a middle-aged County Council labourer, as ridiculous as Madge Dowding dancing on beyond her time.

'I'm waiting outside for you, Cat,' Eyes Horgan called out, lighting a cigarette as he made for the swing-doors.

Already the man with the long arms – made long, so they said, from carrying rocks off his land – had left the ballroom. Others were moving briskly. Mr Dwyer was tidying the chairs.

In the cloakroom the girls put on their coats and said they'd see one another at Mass the next day. Madge Dowding hurried. 'Are you OK, Bridie?' Patty Byrne asked and Bridie said she was.

She smiled at little Patty Byrne, wondering if a day would come for the younger girl also, if one day she'd decide that she was a figure of fun in a wayside ballroom.

'Goodnight so,' Bridie said, leaving the cloakroom, and the girls who were still chatting there wished her goodnight. Outside the cloakroom she paused for a moment. Mr Dwyer was still tidying the chairs, picking up empty lemonade bottles from the floor, setting the chairs in a neat row. His wife was sweeping the floor. 'Goodnight, Bridie,' Mr Dwyer said. 'Goodnight, Bridie,' his wife said.

Extra lights had been switched on so that the Dwyers could see what they were doing. In the glare the blue walls of the ballroom seemed tatty, marked with hair-oil where men had leaned against them, inscribed with names and initials and hearts with arrows through them. The crystal bowl gave out a light that was ineffective in the glare; the bowl was broken here and there, which wasn't noticeable when the other lights weren't on.

'Goodnight so,' Bridie said to the Dwyers. She passed through the swing-doors and descended the three concrete steps on the gravel expanse in front of the ballroom. People were gathered on the gravel, talking in groups, standing with their bicycles. She saw Madge Dowding going off with Tim Daly. A youth rode away with a girl on the crossbar of his bicycle. The engines of motor-cars started.

'Goodnight, Bridie,' Dano Ryan said.

'Goodnight, Dano,' she said.

She walked across the gravel towards her bicycle, hearing Mr Maloney somewhere behind her, repeating that no matter how you looked at it the cement factory would be a great thing for Kilmalough. She heard the bang of a car door and knew it was Mr Swanton banging the door of Mr Maloney's car because he always gave it the same loud bang. Two other doors banged as she reached her bicycle and then the engine started up and the headlights went on. She touched the two tyres of the bicycle to make certain she hadn't a puncture. The wheels of Mr Maloney's car traversed the gravel and were silent when they reached the road.

'Goodnight, Bridie,' someone called, and she replied, pushing her bicycle towards the road.

'Will I ride a little way with you?' Bowser Egan asked.

They rode together and when they arrived at the hill for which it was necessary to dismount she looked back and saw in the distance the four coloured bulbs that decorated the façade of the Ballroom of Romance. As she watched, the lights went out, and she imagined Mr Dwyer pulling the metal grid across the front of his property and locking the two padlocks that secured it. His wife would be waiting with the evening's takings, sitting in the front of their car.

'D'you know what it is, Bridie,' said Bowser Egan, 'you were never looking better than tonight.' He took from a pocket of his suit the small bottle of whiskey he had. He uncorked it and drank some and then handed it to her. She took it and drank. 'Sure, why wouldn't you?' he said, surprised to see her drinking because she never had in his company before. It was an unpleasant taste, she considered, a taste she'd experienced only twice before, when she'd taken whiskey as a remedy for toothache. 'What harm would it do you?' Bowser Egan said as she raised the bottle again to her lips. He reached out a hand for it, though, suddenly concerned lest she should consume a greater share than he wished her to.

She watched him drinking more expertly than she had. He would always be drinking, she thought. He'd be lazy and useless, sitting in the kitchen with the *Irish Press*. He'd waste money buying a secondhand motor-car in order to drive into the town to go to the public houses on fair-days.

'She's shook these days,' he said, referring to his mother. 'She'll hardly last two years, I'm thinking.' He threw the empty whiskey bottle into the ditch and lit a cigarette. They pushed their bicycles. He said:

'When she goes, Bridie, I'll sell the bloody place up. I'll sell the pigs and the whole damn one and twopence worth.' He paused in order to raise the cigarette to his lips. He drew in smoke and exhaled it. 'With the cash that I'll get I could improve some place else, Bridie.'

They reached a gate on the left-hand side of the road and automatically they pushed their bicycles towards it and leaned them against it. He climbed over the gate into the field and she climbed after him. 'Will we sit down here, Bridie?' he said, offering the suggestion as one that had just occurred to him, as though they'd entered the field for some other purpose.

'We could improve a place like your own one,' he said, putting his right arm around her shoulders. 'Have you a kiss in you, Bridie?' He kissed her, exerting pressure with his teeth. When his mother died he would sell his farm and spend the money in the town. After that he would think of getting married because he'd have nowhere to go, because he'd want a fire to sit at and a woman to cook food for him. He kissed her again, his lips hot, the sweat on his cheeks sticking to her. 'God, you're great at kissing,' he said.

She rose, saying it was time to go, and they climbed over the gate again. 'There's nothing like a Saturday,' he said. 'Goodnight to you so, Bridie.'

He mounted his bicycle and rode down the hill, and she pushed hers to the top and then mounted it also. She rode through the night as on Saturday nights for years she had ridden and never would ride again because she'd reached a certain age. She would wait now and in time Bowser Egan would seek her out because his mother would have died. Her father would probably have died also by then. She would marry Bowser Egan because it would be lonesome being by herself in the farmhouse.

The Hill Bachelors

In the kitchen of the farmhouse she wondered what they'd do about her, what they'd suggest. It was up to them; she couldn't ask. It wouldn't be seemly to ask, it wouldn't feel right.

She was a small woman, spare and wiry, her mourning clothes becoming her. At sixty-eight she had ailments: arthritis in her knuckles and her ankles, though only slightly a nuisance to her; a cataract she was not yet aware of. She had given birth without much difficulty to five children, and was a grandmother to nine. Born herself far from the hills that were her home now, she had come to this house forty-seven years ago, had shared its kitchen and the rearing of geese and hens with her husband's mother, until the kitchen and the rearing became entirely her own. She hadn't thought she would be left. She hadn't wanted it. She didn't now.

He walked into the hills from where the bus had dropped him on the main road, by Caslin's petrol pumps and shop across the road from the Master McGrath Bar and Lounge, owned by the Caslins also. It was midday and it was fine. After four hours in two different buses he welcomed the walk and the fresh air. He had dressed himself for the funeral so that he wouldn't have to bring the extra clothes in a suitcase he'd have had to borrow. Overnight necessities were in a ragged blue shopping bag which, every working day, accompanied him in the cab of the lorry he drove, delivering sacks of flour to the premises of bakers, and cartons of pre-packed bags to retailers.

Everything was familiar to him: the narrow road, in need of repair for as long as he had known it, the slope rising gently at first, the hills in the far distance becoming mountains, fields and conifers giving way to marsh and a growth that couldn't be identified from where he walked but which he knew was fern, then heather and bog cotton with here and there a patch of grass. Not far below the skyline were the corrie lakes he had never seen.

He was a dark-haired young man of twenty-nine, slightly made, pink cheeks and a certain chubbiness about his features giving him a genial, easygoing air. He was untroubled as he walked on, reflecting only that a drink and a packet of potato crisps at the Master McGrath might have been a good idea. He wondered how Maureen Caslin had turned out; when they were both fifteen he'd thought the world of her.

At a crossroads he turned to the left, on to an unmade-up boreen, scarcely more than a track. Around him there was a silence he remembered also, quite different from the kind of silence he had become used to in or around the midland towns for which, eleven years ago, he had left these hills. It was broken when he had walked another mile by no more than what seemed like a vibration in the air, a faint disturbance that might have been, at some great distance, the throb of an aeroplane. Five minutes later, rust-eaten and muddy, a front wing replaced but not yet painted, Hartigan's old red Toyota clattered over the potholes and the tractor tracks. The two men waved to each other and then the ramshackle car stopped.

'How're you, Paulie?' Hartigan said.

'I'm all right, Mr Hartigan. How're you doing yourself?'

Hartigan said he'd been better. He leaned across to open the passenger door. He said he was sorry, and Paulie knew what he meant. He had wondered if he'd be in luck, if Hartigan would be coming back from Drunbeg this midday. A small, florid man, Hartigan lived higher up in the hills with a sister who was more than a foot taller than he was, a lean, gangling woman who liked to be known only as Miss Hartigan. On the boreen there were no other houses.

'They'll be coming back?' Hartigan enquired above the rasping noise of the Toyota's engine, referring to Paulie's two brothers and two sisters.

'Ah, they will surely.'

'He was out in the big field on the Tuesday.'

Paulie nodded. Hartigan drove slowly. It wasn't a time for conversation, and that was observed.

'Thanks, Mr Hartigan,' Paulie said as they parted, and waved when the Toyota drove on. The sheepdogs barked at him and he patted their heads, recognising the older one. The yard was tidy. Hartigan hadn't said he'd been down lending a hand but Paulie could tell he had. The back door was open, his mother expecting him.

'It's good you came back,' she said.

He shook his head, realising as soon as he had made it that the gesture was too slight for her to have noticed. He couldn't not have come back. 'How're you doing?' he said.

'All right. All right.'

They were in the kitchen. His father was upstairs. The others would come and then the coffin would be closed and his father would be taken to the church. That was how she wanted it: the way it always was when death was taken from the house.

'It was never good between you,' she said.

'I'd come all the same.'

Nothing was different in the kitchen: the same green paint, worn away to the timber at two corners of the dresser and around the latch of the doors that led to the yard and to the stairs; the same delft seeming no more chipped or cracked on the dresser shelves, the big scrubbed table, the clutter on the smoky mantelshelf above the stove, the uncomfortable chairs, the flagged floor, the receipts on the spike in the window.

'Sit with him a while, Paulie.'

His father had always called him Paul, and he was called Paul in his employment, among the people of the midland towns. Paul was what Patsy Finucane called him.

'Go up to him, Paulie. God rest him,' she said, a plea in her tone that bygones should be bygones, that the past should be misted away now that death had come, that prayer for the safe delivery of a soul was what mattered more.

'Will they all come together?' he asked, still sitting there. 'Did they say that?'

'They'll be here by three. Kevin's car and one Aidan'll hire.'

He stood up, his chair scraping on the flagstones. He had asked the questions in order to delay going up to his father's bedside. But it was what she wanted, and what she was saying without saying it was that it was what his father wanted also. There would be forgiveness in the bedroom, his own spoken in a mumble, his father's taken for granted.

He took the rosary she held out to him, not wishing to cause offence.

Hearing his footsteps on the brief, steeply pitched stairs, hearing the bedroom door open and close, the footsteps again in the room above her, then silence, she saw now what her returned son saw: the bloodless pallor, the stubble that had come, eyelids drawn, lips set, the grey hair she had combed. Frances had been the favourite, then Mena; Kevin was approved of because he was reliable; Aidan was the first-born. Paulie hadn't been often mentioned.

There was the sound of a car, far back on the boreen. A while it would take to arrive at the farmhouse. She set out cups and saucers on the table, not hurrying. The kettle had boiled earlier and she pushed it back on to the hot plate of the stove. Not since they were children had they all been back at the same time. There wouldn't be room for them for the two nights they'd have to spend, but they'd have their own ideas about how to manage that. She opened the back door so that there'd be a welcome.

Paulie looked down at the stretched body, not trusting himself to address it in any way. Then he heard the cars arriving and crossed the room to the window. In the yard Frances was getting out of one and the other was being backed so that it wouldn't be in the way, a white Ford he'd never seen before. The window was open at the top and he could hear the voices, Kevin saying it hadn't been a bad drive at all and Aidan agreeing. The Ford was hired,

Cahill of Limerick it said on a sticker; picked up at Shannon it would have been.

The husbands of Paulie's sisters hadn't come, maybe because of the shortage of sleeping space. They'd be looking after the Dublin children, and it seemed that Kevin's Sharon had stayed behind with theirs in Carlow. Aidan had come on his own from Boston. Paulie had never met Aidan's wife and Sharon only once; he'd never met any of the children. They could have managed in a single car, he calculated, watching his brothers and sisters lifting out their suitcases, but it might have been difficult to organise, Kevin having to drive round by Shannon.

His brothers wore black ties, his sisters were in mourning of a kind, not entirely, because that could wait till later. Mena looked pregnant again. Kevin had a bald patch now. Aidan took off the glasses he had worn to drive. Their suitcases weren't heavy. You could tell there was no intention to stay longer than was necessary.

Looking down into the yard, Paulie knew that an assumption had already been made, as he had known it in the kitchen when he sat there with his mother. He was the bachelor of the family, the employment he had wasn't much. His mother couldn't manage on her own.

He had known it in Meagher's back bar when he told Patsy Finucane he had a funeral to go to. The death had lost him Patsy Finucane: it was her, not his father, he thought about when he heard of it, and in Meagher's the stout ran away with him and he spoke too soon. 'Jeez,' she said, 'what would I do in a farmhouse!'

Afterwards – when the journey through the hills had become a funeral procession at the edge of the town, when the coffin had been delivered to its night's resting place, and later when the burial was complete and the family had returned to the farmhouse and had dispersed the next morning – Paulie remained.

He had not intended to. He had hoped to get a lift in one of the two cars, and then to take a bus, and another bus, as he had on his journey over.

'Where is it they'll separate?' his mother asked in the quietness that followed the departure.

He didn't know. Somewhere that was convenient; in some town they would pull in and have a drink, different now that they weren't in a house of mourning. They would exchange news it hadn't seemed right to exchange before. Aidan would talk about Boston, offering his sisters and his brother hospitality there.

'Warm yourself at the fire, Paulie.'

'Wait till I see to the heifers first.'

'His boots are there.'

'I know.'

His brothers had borrowed the gum boots, too; wherever you went, you needed them. Kevin had fixed a fence, Aidan had got the water going again in the pipe up to the sheep. Between them, they'd taken the slack out of the barbed wire beyond the turf bog.

'Put on a waterproof, Paulie.'

It wasn't going to rain, but the waterproof kept the wind out. Whenever he remembered the farmhouse from his childhood it was windy – the fertiliser bags blowing about in the yard, blustery on the track up to the sheep hills, in the big field that had been the family's mainstay ever since his father had cleared the rocks from it, in the potato field. Wind, more than rain or frost, characterised the place, not that there wasn't a lot of rain too. But who'd mind the rain? his father used to say.

The heifers didn't need seeing to, as he had known they wouldn't. They stood, miserably crouched in against the wall of a fallen barn, mud that the wind had dried hanging from them. His father had taken off the roof when one of the other walls had collapsed, needing the corrugated iron for somewhere else. He'd left the standing wall for the purpose the heifers put it to now.

Paulie, too, stood in the shelter of the wall, the puddles at his feet not yet blown dry, as the mud had on the animals. He remembered the red roof lifted down, piece by piece, Kevin waiting below to receive it, Aidan wrenching out the bolts. He had backed the tractor, easing the trailer close to where they were. 'What's he want it for?' he'd asked Kevin, and Kevin said the corrugated iron would be used for filling the gaps in the hedges.

Slowly, Paulie walked back the way he had come. 'D'you think of coming back?' Aidan had said, saying it in the yard when they were alone. Paulie had known it would be said and had guessed it would be Aidan who'd say it, Aidan being the oldest. 'I'm only mentioning it,' Aidan had said. 'I'm only touching on it.'

Blowing at the turf with the wheel-bellows, she watched the glow spread, sparks rising and falling away. It hadn't been the time to make arrangements or even to talk about them. Nothing could have been more out of place, and she was glad they realised that. Kevin had had a word with Hartigan after the funeral, something temporary fixed up, she could tell from the gestures.

They'd write. Frances had said she would, and Aidan had. Sharon would write for Kevin, as she always did. Mena would. Wherever it was they stopped to say good-bye to one another they'd talk about it and later on they'd write.

'Sit down, Paulie, sit down,' she said when her son came in, bringing the cold with him.

She said again that Father Kinally had done it beautifully. She'd said so yesterday to her daughters in the car, she'd said it to Kevin and to Aidan this morning. Paulie would have heard, yet you'd want to repeat it. You felt the better for it.

'Ah, he did,' Paulie said. 'He did of course.'

He'd taken over. She could feel he'd taken over, the way he'd gone out to see were the heifers all right, the way it was he who remembered, last evening and this morning, that there was the bit of milking to do, that he'd done it without a word. She watched him ease off the gum boots and set them down by the door. He hung the waterproof on the door hook that was there for it and came to the fire in his socks, with his shoes in one hand. She turned away so that he wouldn't notice she'd been reminded of his father coming into the kitchen also.

'Aren't the heifers looking good?' she said.

'Oh, they are, they are.'

'He was pleased with them this year.'

'They're not bad, all right.'

'Nothing's fetching at the minute, all the same.'

He nodded. He naturally would know times were bad, neither sheep nor cattle fetching what they were a year ago, everything gone quiet, the way you'd never have believed it.

'We're in for the night so,' she said.

'We are.'

She washed the eggs Mena had collected earlier, brushing off the marks on them, then wiped the shells clean before she piled them in the bowl. The eggs would keep them going, with the rashers left over and half a saucepan of stew in the fridge. 'You've enough for an army!' Kevin had said, looking into the deep-freeze, and she reminded him you had to have enough in case the weather came in bad.

'What'd we do without it?' she said now, mentioning the deep-freeze. They'd had half a pig from the Caslins, only a portion of the belly used up so far. 'And mutton till Doomsday,' she said.

'How're they these days, the Caslins? I didn't notice Maureen at the funeral.'

'Maureen married a man in Tralee. She's there since.'

'Who's the man?'

'He's in a shoe shop.'

They could have gone to the wedding only it had been a period of the year when you wouldn't want to spare the time. The Hartigans had gone. They'd have taken her but she'd said no.

'Hartigan came back drunk, you should have seen the cut of him! And herself with a frost on her that would have quenched the fire!'

'He's driving down in the morning. He'll pick me up.'

Rashers and black pudding and fried bread were ready on the pan. She cracked two eggs into the fat, turned them when they were ready because he liked them turned. When she placed the plate in front of him he took a mouthful of tea before he ate anything. He said:

'You couldn't manage. No way.'

'It wasn't a time to talk about it, Paulie.'

'I'll come back.'

He began to eat, the yolk of the eggs spreading yellow on the plate. He left the black pudding and the crisp fat of the bacon until last. He'd always done that.

'Hartigan'd still come down. I'm all right on the bit of milking. I'm all right on most things. The Caslins would come up.'

'You couldn't live like that.'

'They're neighbours, Paulie. They got help from himself if they wanted it. I looked over and saw Kevin having a word with Hartigan in the graveyard. It won't be something for nothing, not with Hartigan. Kevin'll tell me later.'

'You'd be dependent.'

'You have your own life, Paulie.'

'You have what there is.'

He ate for several minutes in silence, then he finished the tea that had been poured for him.

'I'd have to give in notice. I'd have to work the notice out. A month.'

'Think it over before you'll do anything, Paulie.'

Paulie harboured no resentment, not being a person who easily did: going back to the farmhouse was not the end of the world. The end of the world had been to hear, in Meagher's back bar, that life on a farm did not attract Patsy Finucane.

As soon as he'd mentioned marriage that day he knew he shouldn't have. Patsy Finucane had taken fright like a little young greyhound would. She'd hardly heard him when he said, not knowing what else to say, 'Ah well, no matter.' It was a nervousness mixed in with the stout that had caused him to make the suggestion, and as soon as he had there was no regaining her: before she looked away that was there in her soft grey eyes. 'I won't go back so,' he'd said, making matters worse. 'I won't go back without you.'

When they sat again in Meagher's back bar after the funeral Paulie tried to put things right; he tried to begin again, but it wasn't any good. During the third week of his working out his notice Patsy Finucane began to go out with a clerk from the post office.

In the yard she threw down grains for the hens and remembered doing it for the first time, apprehensive then about what she'd married into. Nor had her apprehension been misplaced: more than she'd imagined, her position in the household was one of obedience and humility, and sometimes what was said, or incidents that occurred, left a sting that in private drew tears from her. Yet time, simply in passing, transformed what seemed to be immutable. Old age enfeebled on the one hand; on the other, motherhood nurtured confidence. In the farmhouse, roles were reversed.

She didn't want distress like that for any wife Paulie would eventually bring to the kitchen and the house. She would make it easier, taking a back seat from the start and be glad to do so. It was only a pity that Maureen Caslin had married the shoe-shop man, for Maureen Caslin would have suited him well. There were the sisters, of course.

During the weeks that followed Paulie's departure, the anticipated letters came from Mena and Frances and from her daughter-in-law Sharon on behalf of Kevin, and from Aidan. The accumulated content was simple, the unstated expectation stated at last, four times over in different handwriting. Aidan said he and Paulie had had a talk about it. *You are good to think of me*, she wrote back, four times also.

Hartigan continued to come down regularly and a couple of times his sister accompanied him, sitting in the kitchen while he saw to any heavy work in the yard. 'Would Mena have room for you?' she enquired on one of these occasions, appearing to forget that Paulie was due to return when he'd worked out his notice. Miss Hartigan always brought sultana bread when she came and they had it with butter on it. 'I only mentioned Mena,' she said, 'in case Paulie wouldn't be keen to come back. I was thinking he maybe wouldn't.'

'Why's that, Miss Hartigan?'

'It's bachelors that's in the hills now. Like himself,' Miss Hartigan added, jerking her bony head in the direction of the yard, where her brother was up on a ladder, fixing a gutter support.

'Paulie's not married either, though.'

'That's what I'm saying to you. What I'm saying is would he want to stop that way?'

Miss Hartigan's features were enriched by a keenness to say more, to inform and explain, to dispel the bewilderment she had caused. She did so after a pause, politely reaching for a slice of sultana bread. It might not have been noticed that these days the bachelors of the hills found it difficult to attract a wife to the modest farms they inherited.

'Excuse me for mentioning it,' Miss Hartigan apologised before she left.

It was true, and it had been noticed and often remarked upon. Hartigan himself, twenty years ago, was maybe the first of the hill bachelors: by now you could count them – lone men, some of them kept company by a mother or a sister – on the slopes of Coumpeebra, on Slievenacoush, on Knockrea, on Luirc, on Clydagh.

She didn't remember putting all that from her mind when Paulie had said he would come back, but perhaps she had. She tried not to think about it, comforting herself that what had been said, and the tone of Miss Hartigan's voice, had more to do with Miss Hartigan and her brother than with the future in a neighbouring farmhouse. Nor did it necessarily need to be that what had already happened would continue to happen. The Hartigans' stretch of land was worse by a long way than the land lower down on the hill; no better than the side of Slievenacoush, or Clydagh or Coumpeebra. You did the best you could, you hoped for warm summers. Paulie was a good-looking, decent boy; there was no reason at all why he wouldn't bring up a family here as his father had.

'There's two suitcases left down with the Caslins,' he said when he walked in one Saturday afternoon. 'When I get the car started I'll go down for them.'

They didn't embrace; there'd never been much of that in the family. He sat down and she made tea and put the pan on. He told her about the journey, how a woman had been singing on the first of the two buses, how he'd fallen asleep on the second. He was serious the way he told things, his expression intent, sometimes not smiling much. He'd always been like that.

'Hartigan started the car a while back,' she said, 'to make sure it was in form.'

'And it was? All right?'

'Oh, it was, it was.'

'I'll take a look at it later.'

He settled in easily, and she realised as he did so that she had never known him well. He had been lost to her in the family, his shadowy place in it influenced by his father's lack of interest in him. She had never protested about that, only occasionally whispering a surreptitious word or two of comfort. It was fitting in a way that a twist of fate had made him his father's inheritor.

As if he had never been away, he went about his daily tasks knowledgeably and efficiently. He had forgotten nothing – about the winter feed for the heifers, about the work around the yard or where the fences might give way on the hills or how often to go up there after the sheep, about keeping the tractor right. It seemed, which she had not suspected before, that while his presence was so often overlooked he had watched his father at work more conscientiously than his brothers had. 'He'd be proud of you these days,' she said once, but Paulie did not acknowledge that and she resisted making the remark again. The big field, which had been his father's pride, became his. There was another strip to the south of it that could be cleared and reclaimed, he said, and he took her out to show her where he would run the new wall. They stood in the sunshine on a warm June morning while he pointed and talked about it, the two sheepdogs obedient by him. He was as good with them as his father ever had been.

He drove her, as his father had, every three weeks down to Drunbeg, since she had never learnt to drive herself. His father used to wait in the car park of Conlon's Supermarket while she shopped, but Paulie always went in with her. He pushed the trolley and sometimes she gave him a list and he added items from the shelves. 'Would we go and see that?' he suggested one time when they were passing the Two-Screen Rialto, which used to be just the Picture House before it was given a face-lift. She wouldn't be bothered, she said. She'd never been inside the cinema, either in the old days or since it had become a two-screen; the television was enough for her. 'Wouldn't you take one of the Caslin girls?' she said.

He took the older of them, Aileen, and often after that he drove down in the evenings to sit with her in the Master McGrath. The relationship came to an end when Aileen announced that her sister in Tralee had heard of a vacancy in a newsagent and confectioner's, that she'd been to Tralee herself to be looked over and in fact had been offered the position.

'And did you know she had intentions that way?' Paulie's mother asked him when she heard, and he said he had, in a way. He didn't seem put about, although she had assumed herself that by the look of things Aileen Caslin – stolid and on the slow side – would be the wife who'd come to the farmhouse, since her sister Maureen was no longer available. Paulie didn't talk about it, but quite soon after Aileen's departure he began to take an interest in a girl at one of the pay-outs in Conlon's.

'Wouldn't you bring Maeve out one Sunday?' his mother suggested when the friendship had advanced, when there'd been visits to the two-screen and evenings spent together drinking, as there'd been with Aileen Caslin. Maeve was a fair bit livelier than Aileen; he could do worse.

But Maeve never came to the farmhouse. In Conlon's Paulie took to steering the trolley to one of the other pay-outs even when the queue at hers was shorter. His mother didn't ask why. He had his own life, she kept reminding herself; he had his privacy, and why shouldn't he? 'Isn't he the good boy to you?' Father Kinally remarked one Sunday after Mass when Paulie was turning the car. 'Isn't it grand the way it's turned out for you?'

She knew it was and gratefully gave thanks for it. Being more energetic than his father had been at the end, Paulie worked a longer day, far into the evening when it was light enough.

'I don't know did I ever speak a word to her,' she said when he began to go out with the remaining Caslin daughter. Sensible, she looked.

'Ah, sure, anything,' the youngest of the three Caslin girls always said when Paulie told her what films were on and asked which she'd like to see. When the lights went down he waited a bit before he put an arm around her, as he always had with her sisters and with Maeve. He hadn't been able to wait with Patsy Finucane.

The sensible look that Paulie's mother had noted in Annie Caslin was expressed in a matter-of-fact manner. Sentiment played little part in her stalwart, steady nature. She was the tallest and in a general way the biggest of the three Caslin girls, with black hair that she curled and distinctive features that challenged one another for dominance – the slightly large nose, the wide mouth, the unblinking gaze. Paulie took her out half a dozen times before she confessed that what she wanted to do was to live in a town. She'd had the roadside Master McGrath, she said; she'd had serving petrol at the pumps. 'God, I don't know how you'd stand it up in the bogs,' she said before Paulie had a chance to ask her if she'd be interested in coming up to the farmhouse. Even Drunbeg would do her, she said, and got work six months later in the fertiliser factory.

Paulie asked other girls to go out with him, but by then it had become known that what he was after was marriage. One after another, they made excuses, a fact that Hartigan was aware of when he pulled up the Toyota one morning beside a gateway where Paulie was driving in posts. He didn't say anything, but often Hartigan didn't.

'Will it rain, Mr Hartigan?' Paulie asked him.

'The first time I saw your mammy,' Hartigan said, rejecting a discussion about the weather, 'she was stretching out sheets on the bushes. Six years of age I was, out after a hare.'

'A while ago, all right.'

'Amn't I saying it to you?'

Not understanding the conversation, Paulie vaguely shook his head. He struck the post he was easing into the ground another blow. Hartigan said:

'I'd take the big field off you.'

'Ah no, no.'

That was why he had stopped. It might even have been that he'd driven down specially when he heard the thud of the sledge-hammer on the posts, saying to himself that it was a good time for a conversation.

'I wouldn't want to sell the field, Mr Hartigan.'

'But wouldn't you do well all the same if you did? Is it a life at all for a young fellow?'

Paulie didn't say anything. He felt the post to see if it was steady yet. He struck it again, three times before he was satisfied.

'You need a bit of company, boy,' Hartigan said before he backed into the gateway and drove up the hill again.

What she had succeeded in keeping at bay since Miss Hartigan had spoken of it was no longer possible to evade. When Paulie told her about Patsy Finucane she was pleased that he did, glad that he didn't keep it to himself. She knew about everything else: it was all of a piece that Hartigan was trying to get the land cheap by taking advantage of the same circumstances that had left him a bachelor himself. Who could blame him? she said to herself, but even so she wondered if Paulie – so agreeable and good-hearted – would become like that in his time; if he'd become hard, as his father had been, and as grasping as Hartigan.

'I'll go to Mena,' she said. 'There's room there.'

'Ah, there isn't.'

'They'd fit me in.'

'It's here there's room.'

'You want to be married, Paulie. Any man does.'

'He'd take a day shifting a boulder with the tractor. He'd put a ditch through the marsh to gain another half yard. He never minded how long a thing took.'

'It's now we're talking about, Paulie.'

'There'd be sheep in this house within a twelvemonth if Hartigan had it, the doors taken off and made use of, and the next thing is the wind'd be shifting the slates. There'd be grazing taken out of the big field until there wasn't a blade of grass left standing. The marsh'd come in again. No one'd lift a finger.'

'You didn't know what you were coming back to.'

'Ah, I did. I did.'

Obligingly, he lied. You'd say to yourself he was easygoing. When he'd told her about the Finucane girl he'd said it was the way things were. No matter, he'd said. Often you'd forget he wasn't easygoing at all; often she did.

'There's no need, Paulie.'

'There is.'

He said it quietly, the two words hanging there after he had spoken, and she realised that although it was her widowhood that had brought him back it wasn't her widowhood that made him now insist he must remain. She could argue for ever and he would not go now.

'You're good, Paulie,' she said, since there was nothing else left to say.

He shook his head, his dark hair flopping from side to side. 'Errah, no.'

'You are. You are, Paulie.'

When her own death came, her other children would return, again all at the same time. The coffin would be carried down the steep stairs, out into the van in the yard, and the funeral would go through the streets of Drunbeg, and the next day there'd be the Mass. They'd go away then, leaving Paulie in the farmhouse.

'Wait till I show you,' he said, and he took her out to where he was draining another half yard. He showed her how he was doing it. He showed her the temporary wall he had put up, sheets of red corrugated that had come from the old shed years ago.

'That's great,' she said. 'Great, Paulie.'

A mist was coming in off the hills, soft and gentle, the clouds darkening above it. The high edge of Slievenacoush was lost. Somewhere over the boglands a curlew cried.

'Go in out of the drizzle,' he said, when they had stood there for a few minutes.

'Don't stay out long yourself, Paulie.'

Guilt was misplaced, goodness hardly came into it. Her widowing and the mood of a capricious time were not of consequence, no more than a flicker in a scheme of things that had always been there. Enduring, unchanging, the hills had waited for him, claiming one of their own.

He just wanted a decent book to read ...

Not too much to ask, is it? It was in 1935 when Allen Lane, Managing Director of Bodley Head Publishers, stood on a platform at Exeter railway station looking for something good to read on his journey back to London. His choice was limited to popular magazines and poor-quality paperbacks – the same choice faced every day by the vast majority of readers, few of whom could afford hardbacks. Lane's disappointment and subsequent anger at the range of books generally available led him to found a company – and change the world.

'We believed in the existence in this country of a vast reading public for intelligent books at a low price, and staked everything on it'
Sir Allen Lane, 1902–1970, founder of Penguin Books

The quality paperback had arrived – and not just in bookshops. Lane was adamant that his Penguins should appear in chain stores and tobacconists, and should cost no more than a packet of cigarettes.

Reading habits (and cigarette prices) have changed since 1935, but Penguin still believes in publishing the best books for everybody to enjoy. We still believe that good design costs no more than bad design, and we still believe that quality books published passionately and responsibly make the world a better place.

So wherever you see the little bird – whether it's on a piece of prize-winning literary fiction or a celebrity autobiography, political tour de force or historical masterpiece, a serial-killer thriller, reference book, world classic or a piece of pure escapism – you can bet that it represents the very best that the genre has to offer.

Whatever you like to read – trust Penguin.

read more
www.penguin.co.uk